AMANDA
MIRANDA

AMANDA MIRANDA

RICHARD PECK

DIAL BOOKS
NEW YORK

Published by Dial Books
A division of Penguin Putnam Inc.
345 Hudson Street
New York, New York 10014

Copyright ©1980, 1999 by Richard Peck
All rights reserved
Designed by Julie Rauer
Printed in the U.S.A. on acid-free paper
1 3 5 7 9 10 8 6 4 2

This is an abridged edition of *Amanda/Miranda,* originally
published by Viking Books, 1980.

Library of Congress Cataloging in Publication Data
Peck, Richard, date.
Amanda/Miranda / Richard Peck.—Rev.
p. cm.
Summary on file.
ISBN 0-8037-2489-6
[1. Impersonation—Fiction. 2. Mistaken identity—Fiction.
3. England—Social life and customs—20th century—Fiction.
4. Titanic (Steamship)—Fiction.] I. Title.
PZ7.P338Am 1999 [Fic]—dc21 99-12246 CIP AC

To CINDY KANE,
FROM LIFEBOAT NO. 4

PROLOGUE

The Wisewoman lived in the last soft fold of earth before the sea. Some said her rude cottage on the Isle of Wight was built from the stones of the ancients. Stones that once lay on Ashey Down in patterns that only the prehistoric priests could read.

But the folklore was false. The rough rock walls of the Wisewoman's house had never been ancient altars, though they glowed gray with mystery in the hill twilights.

A century earlier the Wisewoman would have been burned as a witch. But the new twentieth century had dawned, bringing a breath of change even to this island, where once the old Queen Victoria had been happiest. But the small woman who had ruled an empire was gone. Her royal Osborne House, not ten miles from the Wisewoman's garden gate, was sealed, and her century had slipped into history.

Smoke from the long liners to America blackened the horizon. Their tall prows knifed out of Southampton port across the narrow water called The Solent to conquer the ice-strewn Atlantic. The world beyond this tiny island that clung to England seemed to stir, sending a ripple of anticipation back across the crouching velvet hills.

And so the Wisewoman wasn't burned or hounded out of her home. She was allowed to live, though not in peace. For she figured in the nightmares of all the local children, and they in hers. By day they dared one another to advance on her cottage. When they supposed that dusk hid them, the bolder ones crept through the Wisewoman's tangled garden and threw small stones at her roof. Often enough she spied them from her crooked window: a dozen urchin faces, pale as cabbages sprouting down her garden rows.

But the Wisewoman was not easily frightened. First and last, she was a businesswoman and the least superstitious soul on the Isle of Wight. She turned a handy profit in the herbs and roots that any cottager might raise in a shady dooryard garden. And she harvested her crops by moonlight only because her customers expected it of her.

As a brewer of home remedies, the Wisewoman was not remarkable. What she could do really well was to foretell the future. More than once she had foreseen in a lovesick lad, creeping to her door for a love potion, the precise moment of his death, though it be forty years in his future.

Once a gaggle of young girls dared each other up the Wisewoman's flagstone path, intent on having their fortunes told. Instead of being assailed by the fumes of a witch's brew, the girls were settled in a row on a bench and offered tea in thin china cups. They soon went their way, none the wiser about their futures. It was the Wisewoman's plan, for she saw early death clinging to the oldest child and would neither lie to her nor frighten her.

There was, the Wisewoman reasoned, no market for this sort of knowledge. Therefore she never turned a profit from prophecy. Only once, startled by a stranger at her door, did she break silence to speak in baffling language of the young woman's future.

Rattling down Nansen Hill, the wagon driven by Josiah Cooke grazed the railing on Dunnose Bridge. The old plow horse staggered but strained on, over the hump of the bridge into the easier dust of the road. But the rusting linchpin on the rear wheel had worked loose. Twenty paces on, it fell free, and the wagon collapsed.

Josiah was pitched off his high perch and sent sprawling across the horse's broad rump. His wife shrieked once, and two shapeless legs in much-mended black stockings flailed the air as she slipped sideways into a mound of bright wildflowers. Mary Cooke, wedged between her parents, slid more slowly to earth and joined her mother.

They were a hardy trio, no strangers to trouble. Mrs. Cooke leaped to her feet, adjusting her black skirts—and Mary's. Josiah untangled himself from the hind legs of the horse and gazed without hope at the wagon, the only thing he owned outright in the world, sagging half in the ditch.

Their only luck was that they were in sight of Bonchurch, on the seaward side of the island. Josiah Cooke trudged off toward the village in search of a wagonman who might spare him a mallet and a linchpin. Mrs. Cooke settled against the flowery bank and gave way to her usual complaints. There was hardly a hint of autumn in the breeze blowing up from the Channel. Still, she pulled her shawl up to her eyes.

"Stand back from the road where you won't be seen, Mary!" she barked. "Then tuck up your skirts, you simple baggage! How will it look to arrive at your first job grass stained? Though at this rate we'll never see Nettlecombe this day, and then where will you be, I should like to know."

Mary Cooke gladly withdrew from her mother. She strolled into the field, her skirts held above her shoe tops, though no strangers were passing on the road to be inflamed by her beauty. Because she never answered back, she didn't mention that even on foot they could reach Nettlecombe before dark. Then Mary would have the opportunity to exchange one bondage for another.

She walked with quickening steps across the unmown grass until her mother's whining voice was lost in the Channel winds. A sudden gust tugged at Mary's black hair, anchored in a severe knot. Had she dared, she would have raced against the wind until she was in sight of the sea. Instead, she wandered with her thoughts.

Mary Cooke had lived all her eighteen years at Whitely Bank, the farmers' village that stands where the roads to Shanklin and Ventnor cross. Both these rough roads lead finally to the sea, and she had forever felt the restless tides stirring inside herself. But she'd never more than glimpsed the green-gold waves that scalloped the beaches of the seaside towns. And it wasn't the carnival atmosphere of the resort towns Mary dreamed of. She'd been reared to shun pleasure. It was the restless, rolling sea itself that flooded her dreams, sometimes beckoning her to destruction, sometimes to new life. But always its call led her far away. Always.

She wandered on in the September stillness. For when her mother and father delivered her to Nettlecombe, these drifting moments would surely end.

To fulfill her mother's plan, Mary Cooke was to go into service for the Whitwell family, whose estate stretched west from Nettlecombe. Mrs. Cooke had trained Mary for her lifetime of service as other girls were prepared for their wedding days. "Someday," her mother would say in a voice grown strangely soft, "you will serve a great family in a fine house."

And so in the cramped cottage where Josiah Cooke sheltered his small family, Mary was taught to serve. She learned to set a proper table, and to carry a heavy tray and open a thick door with her free hand, at an age when other girls were too awkward to cross a threshold without sprawling.

And she'd learned silence. To speak of the rebellion that often welled in her throat was unthinkable. But there was little silence in the Cooke household. Mrs. Cooke filled the empty evenings with her endless memories. She had been in service herself, across the water in Hampshire, before marrying a bumpkin who'd buried her at Whitely Bank.

She'd been driven from the proud panorama of a great country house where she was trusted everywhere, from drawing room to attics. Where she took her tea with the governess and the housekeeper themselves. Where her lady called her "my treasure" as she turned back the swansdown sheets.

She had left the rustle of gray silk for the manure-stained tatters of a farmer's wife. All she could hope for now was to create in Mary a servant who might nearly rival herself. There was justice in this, Mrs. Cooke was certain. For Mary was the unwanted child whose coming had forced her to leave her lady's house in hasty disgrace.

"Never," Mrs. Cooke would say at the end of an evening, "never turn your back upon your betters. . . . Always keep your eyes down. . . . Speak clearly when they find it necessary to speak to you. . . . Note their every need."

Mary had been allowed a little schooling, for her mother knew the value of a well-spoken servant. She had learned to read, to write a clear hand, and to add the figures of a household account. She had heard poetry for the first time and was haunted by her teacher's mournful chanting of the verses:

> *Alone, alone, all, all alone,*
> *Alone on a wide, wide sea!*

And Mary had learned to speak in a tone respectful enough to suit the persons of quality, the gods and goddesses she was being shaped to serve.

Now the Whitwells of Nettlecombe were to receive a

new servant. Whether Mary would find her place scouring the roasting pans or dressing the young lady of that house depended very much on the impression she made at the outset.

As she drifted farther from the broken wagon, Mary slipped free of all her hard-learned lessons. She climbed a stile and started up a fold of earth where the tang of salt air grew sharper. She might have appeared to be running away. But there was no place to go. She was at the Wisewoman's cottage before she realized it. The little stone house rose half out of the earth before her eyes. As she noticed the door, it opened.

The Wisewoman could tell at first glance that she was not being visited by a client. And she favored the young girl in the shapeless dress with a formal nod that none of her clients ever got from her.

"I meant no harm. I was only passing," Mary stammered from the front gate. But the quiet tones she'd learned were lost in the singing sea wind.

The Wisewoman nodded again and swept her hand back to the open door, inviting her in. Uncertainly Mary walked up the stepping-stones of a dooryard overgrown with red chickweed.

"You have lost your way, perhaps."

Confused by kindness, Mary only stared at the old woman, whose neck was webbed with wrinkles as fine as ivory lace. The very old woman and the very young one found each other beautiful in a wordless moment. "Lost or certain of your course," the Wisewoman said at last, "come and rest yourself."

To be received like this was beyond Mary's experience. The old woman had to gesture twice before Mary would sit in her presence.

More like a cool cave than a parlor, the cottage's only room served as the Wisewoman's kitchen and pharmacy. Mary's eyes roamed the apothecary bottles lining the walls. Above, the rafters were hung with bunches of drying herbs and heather, pale silver and paler lavender. She wondered at their uses.

The Wisewoman placed a gold-rimmed cup of black tea in the girl's hand. She allowed the silence to lengthen while astonishing images of Mary's future played across her inner eye.

At last, bested by curiosity, Mary asked, "Is this a chemist shop, my lady?"

The question brought the old woman back to earth. She paused a moment, choosing the words to describe her livelihood. "In a manner of speaking. Here there is folk medicine for those who mistrust doctors even more than they mistrust me. But why do you call me 'my lady'?"

Mary went pale with shame. "I—I was taught it was proper."

"You are a servant?" The Wisewoman was amazed, for her visions of the girl's future foretold otherwise.

"By nightfall I shall be," Mary said softly. "At Nettle-combe."

"A servant speaks as you have done only where she is employed. You are not servant to all the world."

The idea, though meant kindly, was strange to Mary, almost meaningless.

"And you will serve until you marry?"

"I—I think I shall never marry, for my mother said—"

"Oh yes! You shall marry twice," said the Wisewoman. She'd been startled into telling the truth she'd foreseen.

Mary thought her mistaken, even though the old woman's knowledge hung heavily about them in this place.

"I can divine the future," the woman explained. "It is an uncertain gift, and I take no credit for it, nor any pay."

"And can you see more about my future?" asked Mary.

After a silence an answer of sorts came. "I am addled by it—and by you. Your future lies a great deal farther off than Nettlecombe. It lies beyond a mountain of ice, where you will die and live again. I see you in a world so strange and distant that the images seem the trickery of a Gypsy's false promises, even to me."

She broke off then, and the two sat motionless until the mantel clock struck noon. As if she'd heard her mother's far-off cry, Mary rose. But at the cottage door the Wisewoman motioned her to wait while she disappeared back into the gloom. Returning, she pressed a cold disc into Mary's hand. "It is for you," said the woman who had never given a gift. "Though it has no magic powers, I believe it should belong to you."

Mary stared down at a coin—foreign but not old. There was the face of some copper savage in worn relief on it. "I found it on the beach one day," the Wisewoman said. "There were other things scattered in the sand, perhaps from a shipwreck. An American ship, I shouldn't wonder, for it's an American coin. Take it back."

Out in the sunshine, Mary turned just as the Wisewoman was closing the door. "When shall I meet the men I shall marry?" she asked, too shamed at her boldness to look up.

"Why, tonight, of course. Both of them." And then, as the Wisewoman watched Mary moving quickly away across the flagstones, almost in flight, she said, "Goodbye . . . Amanda."

But the Channel winds swept the name far out to sea.

A double row of black Italian pines threw long afternoon shadows across the approach to Whitwell Hall. In the great square salon where Lady Eleanor sat with the female members of her house party, the lamps were already lit.

The ladies lingered over their tea, balancing the cups on silken knees, brushing a crumb of tea cake from the folds of their afternoon dresses. Conversation drifted in the last moments before they would have to go up and begin dressing for dinner. If one of them had risen from her chair and glanced out of the long window, she might have noted the Cookes' crippled wagon being dragged over the gravel drive behind the ponderous horse.

The house glowing at the top of the rise seemed vast to Mary, as if an entire village had been gathered neatly under a single roof. Even Mrs. Cooke caught her breath at its magnificence. To cover her awe, she barked at her husband, "Look sharp for a turning to the back of the house, Josiah! Have you no more sense than to fetch up at the front door?"

To Mary she said nothing. She'd left the red marks of

her fingers across her daughter's cheek when the shiftless girl had finally returned from her noontime wandering.

The tall columns of the front portico loomed above them before Josiah found the tradesmen's lane forking to one side. It was hardly more than a slit in the high boxwood, and at once they were swallowed in the near night of the hedgerows. At the end the narrow way widened to a paved yard between the kitchen wing and a jumble of outbuildings. If Josiah's ancient horse had been more alert, it would have shied at a motionless figure standing just off the lane in a gap between hedge and stables.

John Thorne had stood for some time while the shadows crept over him, darkening all but the glints in his straw-blond hair. Only his hands moved as he rubbed with a rag at the grease embedded in his calloused palms. His mind was elsewhere. He stared up at a pair of windows high in the great house, far above the servants' domain. He'd watched reflected sunset wash them red, then purple. And still he stood until another servant would draw the curtains of Miss Amanda Whitwell's room.

The young man had spent the day demolishing the old barn doors on the stable wing. Tomorrow meant hanging the new modern doors he'd paneled himself. The stables were being refitted for the Whitwells' new motorcar. No favorite in the servants' hall, John Thorne was a valuable craftsman who repaired and maintained Whitwell Hall as if every splinter and stone were his own. Now he was to be promoted to chauffeur-mechanic when the new car arrived.

His territory ceased at the kitchen yard. But it stretched back to the outbuildings and the pastures of the home farm to the distant cottage in the grove. He'd been born there before the Whitwells had come.

Just as the curtains on Amanda Whitwell's window were drawn by the invisible hands of one Mrs. Buckle, the Cookes' wagon crunched past the motionless man. Something came over Mary then. Something made her glance back. But she saw only the shadow of a man.

The quiet grounds gave no hint of the bustle inside the house as the dinner hour approached. In the dining room a pair of gaitered footmen, hired for the occasion, hovered over a table set for twenty-four in a blaze of silver and French crystal.

The fanning door to the serving pantry suggested the storm brewing below stairs. The serving maids, Hilda and Hannah and Betty, in caps like overstarched toadstools, rustled past one another.

Below, Mrs. Creeth, the cook and empress of the kitchen, was locking horns—not for the first time—with Mrs. Buckle, the housekeeper whose influence ceased at the door between family and staff. But Mrs. Buckle, whose accents grew hideously refined in her encounters with the lesser servants, had invaded enemy territory at its busiest hour. Now she and Mrs. Creeth stood, each gripping a handle of the same silver tray.

"Give it over, if you *please*, Mrs. Buckle!" Mrs. Creeth shrieked. "There'll be no catering to imaginary invalids until Sir Timothy and Lady Eleanor's guests have ate and drunk their fill!"

White with rage, Mrs. Buckle twisted the tray from the cook's grasp. It swung down to rap her own bony knees. "I haven't any intention of disrupting your culinary efforts," she said, "for I know how very *difficult* it is for you, Mrs. Creeth, to manage even an *ordinary* dinner . . . at your age."

The words fell on Mrs. Creeth like an ether-soaked rag. She fell back, and Mrs. Buckle swept past her to the stove, where she began to coddle an egg and toast a slice of bread for Amanda Whitwell.

Arranging the bland meal on the elaborate tray, the housekeeper sighed. "Poor Miss Amanda, who has hardly known a well day in all her young life. Who would care for her few needs if not her dear old Buckle, who was nurse and nanny to her."

"Just how sick *is* Miss Amanda *this* time?" the cook demanded.

But this rude intrusion was ignored. With maddening calm, Mrs. Buckle turned to Mrs. Creeth and said, "Would you be good enough to locate a silver vase and one perfect rosebud before I take this tray upstairs?"

Mrs. Creeth's lips parted dangerously. But there was a knock at the outside door. Whirling, Mrs. Creeth howled at Betty. "You, girl! See who's at the door!"

Betty made a careful circle around the two women and pulled the door open. There stood Mrs. Cooke and Mary, who carried a small wicker satchel.

Mrs. Cooke took in the scene at a glance. "Where is Mr. Finley?" she demanded in a ringing voice.

At that moment the mighty Mr. Finley, butler above and dictator below, entered. He noted that Mrs. Creeth and Mrs. Buckle were standing nearer one another than was good for either of them. "Ah, Mrs. Cooke, is it not?" he said, advancing to the door.

Mary longed to run then, back to the wagon and her father. But Mr. Finley never glanced at her. He was saying to her mother, "I see you have brought the girl. She is sensible and literate, is she not?"

Mary noticed that Mr. Finley's left nostril vibrated as if it detected a repulsive odor, while the other refused to become involved.

"She is," Mrs. Cooke hastened to say, "trained by me, who once personally attended Lady—"

"Yes, yes, I have no doubt. You have provided her with aprons in good repair and one suitable costume for her afternoon off, if she is granted one?"

"I have," Mrs. Cooke vowed. "The very aprons I myself—"

"Yes." Mr. Finley spoke as a man whose most pressing duties lay elsewhere. But when he finally deigned to look at Mary, he blinked, almost in a baffled kind of recognition. "What are you called?" he asked, after a troubled moment.

"Mary, sir," she murmured, bobbing from the knee.

"Yes. Sensible," he said. "You will find that—"

A cymbal crash and an inhuman howl deafened the kitchen. The battle of wills between Mrs. Buckle and Mrs. Creeth had gone beyond words. Mrs. Buckle had begun her own search for a bud vase in the cupboards above. Mrs. Creeth's hand, sudden as a snake striking, overbalanced the tray on the counter, sending it crashing to the floor.

Weeks of Mrs. Buckle's accumulated dignity lay in ruins at her feet. *"Daughter of the devil!"* she screamed at Mrs. Creeth.

"Enough!" Mr. Finley barked. "Mrs. Buckle, I am astonished at your outburst. Prepare another tray, but you are in no fit state to take it up. You, Mary"—he turned to the girl at the door—"take up Miss Amanda's tray." Mary's mother nudged her sharply.

"Betty." Mr. Finley snapped a finger. "Fetch one of our aprons and a cap and show the new girl how they are worn."

As Mary stepped forward to obey, her mother stepped backward into the yard. Mr. Finley closed the door firmly, cutting Mary off from all she'd ever known.

Amanda Whitwell of Whitwell Hall lay in the center of an oak bed as big as a barge. She was gazing into a hand mirror, enthralled with herself.

Black hair haloed her face in wildly tossed ringlets. She'd powdered her face lightly, artfully. And she thought it a pity she never rouged her lips. Leaving it off now would make her look more like an interesting invalid.

Amanda studied the violet-blue eyes that returned her look. There was a certain sharpness in those eyes that nearly gave her away. But she knew how to soften her gaze. She only had to think of the one man in her world who could almost make her forget all trickery. Her eyes grew dreamy, and she seemed to regain the innocence she'd so gladly lost.

Her healthy complexion glowed softly through the white powder. Searching for flaws, she found none. Almost none. There was the odd little half-moon scar that faintly divided her right eyebrow. Three and a half years before, when she was just fifteen, a docile mare named Sapphire had forgotten its manners and shrugged her off. She'd fallen onto pillow-soft ground, but a small, sharp stone had neatly split her eyebrow in two.

Lady Eleanor had shuddered at how near her daughter

had come to being blinded. And the stable door was forever closed to Amanda, much to her relief, for she preferred the comfort of the new motorcars.

A hesitant knock at the door brought her around. She was used to Mrs. Buckle's sudden entries. Surprised, Amanda hid the mirror. "John?" she called out before she thought. But it was Mary who entered, balancing a silver tray, now slightly bent.

Mary's eyes widened at the room and at the fire burning heartily below a marble mantel. The idea of a warm bedroom was beyond her imaginings. And the girl in the elegant bed seemed someone from a fairy tale.

"Please, miss, your supper tray."

"Well, bring it along, then," Amanda Whitwell said, but then she stared as Mary drew closer. It was a look of naked surprise, such as Mr. Finley had registered. "Put down the tray and take off your cap!"

Wondering, Mary swept off the cap.

"Yes," Amanda mused, "even the same black hair, though better controlled than mine. You don't dye it, do you?"

"Oh no, miss," Mary said, confused.

"Finley dyes his hair," Amanda said. "In his natural state he's as gray as an old rat, I should think. Move the tray closer. What have we here?" Amanda removed a silver cover. "I believe the kitchen is taking the invalid at her word. Who are you?" she said abruptly.

"Mary Cooke, miss."

"That won't do at all. Quite unsuitable. Mary is too ordinary. And the alternative is to call you Cooke, which would suggest Mrs. Creeth. What shall I call you?"

"I don't know, I'm sure, miss."

"Miranda, I think. Yes, Miranda and Amanda. They go nicely together. Would that suit you?"

"I suppose so, miss."

"And so it should. There is a Miranda in *The Tempest*. You know, Shakespeare's play. Miranda is a beautiful heroine, so the matter is decided. Why isn't everything so easy to arrange?"

"I'm sure I don't know, miss." She thought about that. "I suppose everything comes right if we put forth our best efforts."

"Oh, dear, how hearty that sounds." Amanda ran the back of her small hand across her forehead. "I do hope you're not *too* hearty. I have a rather robust friend, and she tires me terribly."

Mary was far out of her depth. She herself had learned a scrap of Shakespeare, but had never heard it brought into conversation. She'd have almost preferred being back in the battlefield of the kitchens.

"You may sit on the bed while I eat, Miranda."

"Oh no, miss," Mary said, shocked. "I couldn't."

"It's obvious that you've been taught to obey. Do so."

Mary lowered herself onto the edge of the bed and didn't know where to look while Amanda wolfed down her small meal.

"I would sell my soul for a wedge of Camembert!" Amanda said.

"Then you're feeling better, Miss Amanda. Shall I slip down to the pantry and bring a plate of—"

"No, no," Amanda said. "I'll play out my hand. You haven't the least notion of what's going on, do you?"

"No, miss." Without meaning to, Mary stared into eyes precisely the same shade as her own.

"I am having a temper tantrum, and the rather complicated reason is that—"

"*You, Mary! On your feet!* The idea!" Mrs. Buckle had made a swift and silent entry. Mary leaped from the bedside.

"Where is your cap, you wicked wanton? To the kitchens, and be quick!" Mrs. Buckle commanded.

"No, she will remain with me," Amanda said in a small, steely voice.

"She'll do nothing of the kind! I won't have this sort of familiarity in—"

"Mrs. Buckle, if she lives another ninety years, she will never equal your familiarity. Yes, I know you nursed and nannied and nagged me from the first. When I'm feeling myself again, I shall remember to be grateful. Until then, please leave Miranda with me."

"And who might *Miranda* be?" Mrs. Buckle bristled. This young maid already threatened her position with Miss Amanda.

"I've renamed the new servant. I trust you have no objections."

Mrs. Buckle smoothed her gray silk front and pursed her lips. "I'm sure my objections would carry very little weight when you are in one of your willful moods, Miss Amanda."

"Right as usual, dear old Buckle. So you may go. I won't be needing you tonight. And do try not to make Miranda's life a torment simply on my account."

"Well, really! As if I would!" said Buckle, withdrawing with as much dignity as she could muster.

"Such an old trout," Amanda said in a ringing voice before the door had quite closed.

"Oh, miss," Mary said, working her hands.

"Yes, a bad beginning, I know. But with Buckle, there is no other kind. You may have noticed that I am easily as willful as Buckle claims. But I am quite nice until someone crosses me. Then I tend to lash out. Oh, *do* sit down again!"

Mary/Miranda settled uneasily on the edge of the bed again. She could hardly think, though her mind was quicker than anyone had ever noticed. Amanda was odd, but Mary found herself cautiously drawn to the girl who seemed very commanding for someone so young. Then Mary noticed the white powder dusted over the innocent-seeming face. It wasn't her place to notice, but Amanda left her little time to consider.

"Have the men returned from Cowes?" she asked. "They went to look at a yacht someone wants to buy. I hate boats, don't you?"

"I couldn't say, Miss Amanda. I've never been on a boat."

"But surely you've crossed to the mainland on the ferry?"

"Oh, never, miss." Mary's eyes grew round. "I've never been off the Isle. Where would I have gone?"

None of the maids—Hilda or Hannah or Betty—had ever been off the Isle of Wight. Only the embattled Buckle and Creeth moved back and forth with the Whitwell family to London.

This sudden glimpse of the bondage of the lower servants unnerved Amanada. She chose not to think about it, saying, "You have not been here long?"

"I only just came, miss."

"Then you haven't met . . . everybody?"

"No, miss."

Amanda came to a small, satisfying decision. "I think I shall want you for my own personal maid. You'll be quite useful to me. After all, I am to have a London Season next summer—if I don't marry first. And we shall certainly be going up to London in November for the Little Season. I'll need more than old Buckle to keep track of my clothes after I've danced until dawn."

"It sounds quite exciting, miss."

"Does it? I suppose so. But pointless if I am to marry Gregory Forrest, which is the current plot afoot. There's no point in dancing with every spotty youth in London if one is to marry an American from New York. One feels quite trapped." She sighed. "And marriage is the worst trap of all. Though perhaps a safe harbor, if something can be both a trap and a harbor. You must see me through, Miranda. I'm feeling rather hopeless now. But mark me! I've been known to spoil other people's meddling plans. *You* aren't thinking of marrying, are you?"

"Oh no, miss." But then Mary remembered the Wise-woman's strange words, and she colored. But a rattling, uncertain knock interrupted her thoughts.

"I cannot *bear* it!" Amanda twitched with temper. "Yes! Who is it?"

It was either Hilda or Hannah looming in the doorway. They were sisters and just alike. "Oh, Miss Amanda, if you please, I was sent to fetch the new one—"

"She's called *Miranda!*" Amanda shouted.

"If you say so, miss."

"I *do* say so!"

"Yes, miss." Hilda—it was Hilda—wiped her nose nervously with the end of her apron. "She's to come help at table. They's as busy as bees in bottles down there and Mr. Finley says—"

"Ah, Finley. Then I suppose you must go," Amanda said to Miranda. "I shall send Miranda along shortly, Hannah."

Hilda sniffed and vanished. Mary adjusted her cap and rose to go. As she lifted the tray from the bed, Amanda's hand grasped her wrist. Lightly, but Mary could feel fingernails imprinting her flesh. "As you serve in the dining room tonight, Miranda, look sharp and notice the young American gentleman. Then tomorrow you can tell me what you think of him. You'll notice him. He's quite divinely handsome and better behaved than the rest. He is the man my mother has decided I should marry."

Mary could only wonder why her young mistress wasn't downstairs dining grandly beside her fiancé.

"But I am a rebel. When I'm deprived of satisfaction, I can usually withhold it from others. Poor Gregory will have to do without me. It will make my mother wild. No, don't worry. I shan't sulk in my bed forever. I'll think of a plan to foil them all."

"But, miss—"

"I know. You wonder why I don't obey my family and make a suitable marriage"—Mary hadn't been nearly bold enough to wonder that—"and I will tell you. I love someone else. Quite hopeless, and quite madly. And if my mother knew who he was, she would in her serene and gracious manner have me flogged."

John Singer Sargent's portrait of Lady Eleanor Whitwell hung at the far end of the double drawing room. Lady Eleanor in court dress—cascading skirts of ivory petals, feathers crowning her hair—at Buckingham Palace in the last year of Queen Victoria's reign. She'd been forty when Sargent completed his work. Now, at fifty-one, she could have sat for the portrait again, her beauty unchanged.

Late summer was the Isle of Wight's only social season, when London society came for the regatta at Cowes. Lady Eleanor stood that long September evening beneath the portrait of herself, entertaining her houseguests and being only a little entertained by them. The gentlemen had returned from Cowes, and so the room was balanced between the blackness of their dinner clothes and the colors of the ladies' gowns.

It had been very different in the previous summer, 1910. Then ladies and gentlemen alike had worn black to mourn the passing of King Edward after his short reign. Now the pall had lifted, and the aristocracy had returned to their pursuit of pleasure.

Lady Eleanor looked across the sea of chattering guests to Gregory Forrest's tall, immaculate figure. He stood patiently, listening to the tedious monologue of her husband, Sir Timothy. She stared at the unlined, open face and the visionary eyes that were pure American. She'd courted this young man on Amanda's behalf in a manner that had raised an occasional eyebrow. But Lady Eleanor, the third daughter of an impoverished duke, was faithful to a fault to the monotonous old Sir Timothy, a tea merchant fifteen years her senior. It was plain what she was about with this handsome American, for he was rich. He was the only son of a beer baron, a German immigrant who had settled in Brooklyn and changed the family name from Wald to Forrest, in celebration of his new citizenship.

People murmured about the mingling of Forrest beer and Whitwell tea. There was even a line or two of bad verse repeated just out of Lady Eleanor's hearing:

> *And malt does more than background can*
> *To justify Amanda's man.*

Lady Eleanor had set Amanda's cap for Gregory Forrest, and headstrong Amanda had seemed to go along with the plan, at least for a time. She'd been only seventeen then and just out of the schoolroom, if it could be said she'd ever been schooled. Her formal introduction to society had still lain a year or two away. And Amanda's beauty already promised much.

Sir Timothy had brought Gregory Forrest home from his London club. They were an unlikely pairing. Sir Timothy, almost deaf, had never been able to converse on any subject but the tea-importing business. Gregory Forrest had listened with the patience of a parish priest while his eye roved and came to rest upon Amanda.

More than his wealth influenced Lady Eleanor. She saw strength in the set of the American's shoulders and determination in his apparently dreamy eyes. She hoped he might exercise a necessary control over Amanda that she as a mother could never manage. There was a dark side to her daughter. The wildest heights of childish merriment could turn to the grimmest sulks. Amanda's rebellion, now playful, might blossom—and soon—into the bright flower of disgrace. Amanda's mother understood her far better than Amanda knew.

The dinner gong sounded at last, striking a brassy note across Lady Eleanor's thoughts. At the far end of the room, Sir Timothy clapped a vague hand on his prospective son-in-law's back and went looking for the lady he was to take in to dinner, a Mrs. Glaslough. And Lady Eleanor was claimed by her dinner partner, a Mr. Harry Emerson, whose alliance with Mrs. Glaslough was often noted in the more disreputable newspapers. Lady Eleanor took Mr. Emerson's arm and led the way to the dining room.

It was an evening's work for Gregory Forrest to concentrate on his dinner partner's conversation. Miss Ward-Benedict, Amanda's special friend, had a great many teeth and a great many pearls, and her hands were covered with antiquated rings. But there was no wedding band among them. She'd long since navigated the choppy seas of an extended mating season—London, Dublin, India—and had reached the far shore unclaimed. She was in every sense a miss.

Gregory was happy enough not to be paired with the notorious Mrs. Glaslough, though her beauty had stood the test of time. But when she spoke, even in an undertone, she was audible four chairs away. And her laughter reminded him of the sparks that sent the new wireless radio messages from ship to ship across the empty sea.

Like anybody with one foot planted in a foreign culture, Gregory Forrest was startled by the folkways. The openness with which illicit romance was treated in England would knock crude New York sideways. Apparently this Mrs. Glaslough and the man on Lady Eleanor's right were always given adjoining rooms when they visited country houses. They passed the days ignoring one another and the nights in one another's arms. It wasn't quite the England of Gregory Forrest's schoolbook history or the Harvard course in British literature.

But his basically romantic soul was ignited by the pageantry here. Every figure around this sumptuous table seemed to fit effortlessly into the pattern. The drooping mustaches above the towering winged collars. The ropes of inherited diamonds and opals adorning softly rounded or pigeon-ponderous breasts. The heads nodding to conversation that moved cleverly to the brink of scandal, then retreated knowingly.

It was all a good deal for a brewer's son to absorb. Gregory's mind retreated to the house where he'd spent his boyhood. To Bushwick in Brooklyn, where the German brewery owners' turreted mansions backed upon their own foremen's wooden row houses. Bushwick, where even the well water seemed to taste of hops. And he remembered his father, who worked beside his laborers in boots and overalls. A brewer born, who could read no English, little German, but every figure in a financial statement.

The most familiar scenes of Gregory Forrest's life glowed suddenly bright, and the most painful memory struck like lightning in his mind. To remember Brooklyn was to remember his best friend, Sammy Bettendorf, the son of a junk-wagon driver.

Greg shared all his secrets with Sammy, and they plotted new lives as Kansas cowboys. Sammy, who lived with his stout parents and four sisters at the top of a frame row house on Goodwin Street.

It was a muggy summer's night in the year Greg turned nine, and his dreams had been only dimly disturbed by the fire engine's bells. In the morning he'd awakened to find his mother sitting on the edge of his bed, her wrapper pulled tight around her. "There vas trouble last night, Greg." She ran her hand through his tousled dark hair. "Bad trouble, my boy, down Goodvin Street."

"Sammy?" Greg asked. "Trouble at the Bettendorfs'?"

She nodded and the tears welled in her eyes. "A fire. It vas very bad. The engines could do nothing." His mother looked at him, trying to tell him with her eyes.

"But Sammy?"

"Sammy and all his family are gone."

"Gone? Dead?" Greg asked at last. "All of them?"

"Ja. All. . . ."

Years later and three thousand miles away, Gregory Forrest's memory probed that moment again and found the wound unhealed. But it brought back other memories of his mother, of her storytelling that had fueled his earliest dreams. Tales of black forests full of helpless widows and useful elves and bright treasures guarded by ogres. And always in the woodland clearing a beautiful maiden whose blond braids coiled around a ravishing face. A chaste, blond, milk-fed beauty awaiting a hero's liberating kiss. Now Gregory Forrest had found quite another old-world maiden. And long after he'd put such boyish romancing behind him.

Foreseeing the family's first gentleman, his father had sent Gregory away to boarding school, then to college where the Arrow-collared sons of older money drank whiskey, not beer. But the old man hadn't reckoned with the intellect that took Gregory to law school, where he finished first in the class of 1909. Or the growing desire for creativity, which drew his son's mind beyond courtrooms—the need to create a life not merely for himself but for the immigrants still pouring into New York.

Gregory Forrest began to dream of houses. Houses to replace the city's terrible tenements where in winter families slept in the warmth of crowded bodies.

When Gregory gave up a place in a Wall Street law firm and announced his intention to study architecture, the old brewer could only shake his head in wonder. But if it was to be housebuilding instead of law, then so be it. After a brief look at the bold beauties of Fifth Avenue society and the tennis-playing sisters of his Harvard classmates, he set out on a grand tour of Europe to examine the architectural triumphs so lacking in New York. The tour was meant only to begin with London. But it had ended there on the day he first saw Sir Timothy's Amanda poised on the sofa in the Whitwells' darkly paneled London drawing room in Charles Street.

He'd fallen in love with her beauty: her black hair still drawn back like a schoolgirl's, her cool violet gaze— in love with everything about her. Even the disturbing sense that she might bolt at any moment, leaving him in the world alone.

Gregory Forrest worked steadily toward the moment when Amanda would stop calling him "Father's friend." But she knew how to dangle herself before him, and then draw back. He experienced the torture of a young man overwhelmed by his own capacity to suffer. He dreamed of making her his wife. Of going back to New York with her. Of rebuilding the sprawling, sordid city: he to plan and carry out, she to inspire and encourage.

When Lady Eleanor reminded him with exquisite tact of Amanda's youth, he contented himself with a more measured courtship. He courted her and her mother and father. He'd have willingly courted all Charles Street and London and the Isle of Wight.

He slipped over to the Continent occasionally, to stir himself with its architectural glories. But he learned that it was easier to be in the same country as Amanda, even when they were separated by geography or her moods. He enrolled himself in a London school of architecture and managed to get through whole days in the pursuit of a subject less elusive than Amanda.

When he grew bold and embraced her almost roughly,

she only laughed. When he was driven into frustrated hopelessness, she grew absentmindedly tender. It took very little to win him back, and Amanda enjoyed the work, though it was only a game to her.

There'd been that August day when Gregory's face had darkened with an anger that warned even Amanda. "Damn it, Amanda, stop playing games. If you want to be a child, go back to your nanny, or whatever she's called. You want all the freedom of a woman and all the protection of a child."

"I was never a child, not really," Amanda said. "That's just the point. While you were roaming the American prairie, having had your independence declared for you, I was a prisoner in the nursery. I was scheming at an age when you were thinking—whatever little boys think about."

"And what was the point of all that scheming?"

"Well, it didn't get me very far, I'm bound to admit. But—oh, don't you see? Doesn't anyone?" Amanda shifted on the long drawing-room sofa where they sat. She drew her legs up, then settled quite companionably with her back resting against Gregory's shoulder. A wisp of her hair swept his cheek, and he knew that whatever this argument was about, he would lose it.

"I want the freedom you men take for granted. But I doubt I'd find that even in the Land of the Free, as you Americans so arrogantly call it. I want to make my own decisions. This is the twentieth century. Yet women are still meant to be decorative by day and compliant by night, while men have cornered the market on freedom of choice."

"Choose me and you'll have exercised all the rights of the New Woman," Gregory said, yearning to draw her into his arms.

"Don't talk down to me, Gregory. What if I *have* chosen someone else already? Has the thought crossed your mind?"

"Has it crossed yours?"

"What pomposity! Perhaps it has."

"Then I doubt that you'd be crying for your freedom."

"Matters are not that cut-and-dried." Then Amanda surprised him by turning to say, "Give me your hand."

He held out his hand and she gripped it in her small fist, rubbing her thumb across it from wrist to fingertip.

"Are you going to read my palm?" he asked, trying to coax her out of this fiery mood.

"I don't need a fortune-teller's powers to see you haven't worked a day in your life."

"Neither have you."

"That's not the point. Behind all your vigorous American idealism, you're as idle as all the men I've ever known. Almost all of them."

"What makes you think I'm an idealist?"

"Heavens! You positively *reek* of idealism. You have some master plan about reforming the world that you mean to spring on me when I've finally given way to your charms and am fainting with love in your arms. It's true, isn't it? I'm never wrong."

If Gregory Forrest hadn't been in love with Amanda Whitwell before, that moment would have turned the tide. This self-centered, icily remote girl had seen through him.

"It's true. There's something I want very much to do—apart from marrying you, Amanda."

"Well, go on. I'm longing to hear what it is."

He told her. Amanda fidgeted, but seemed to hear him out. He told her of the New York teeming with immigrants, of the eternally dark streets, of water unfit to drink, of epidemics that raged from room to crowded room. He nearly told her how the best friend of his boyhood had died in a tinderbox bedroom. He drew back at the last moment, unwilling to relive it himself.

But he told her the dream that was growing in him: to build solid, safe houses with lawns and plumbing and electricity. Streets—neighborhoods of them, free of filth and disease and despair. Free of the shoddy materials that invited death by the fire that came in the night.

Amanda listened—unwillingly. She wasn't shocked by the sufferings of faceless immigrants. She was more disturbed by Gregory Forrest's idealistic plans to give them a better life. He spoke of these people as his fellow citizens. He saw no distance between them and himself. He seemed to view his future as part of theirs. And he meant it.

It surpassed idealism, and left her behind. She could never rule Gregory Forrest, not on her terms. He had a ruling passion already. In the hour that Gregory was falling more deeply in love with her, touched by the silence in which she heard him out, Amanda added one more reason to resist him. It would have been kind to say to him at that moment: You need another sort of woman. Go find her. But Amanda was not kind, and without a suitable suitor, she'd be left at the mercy of her mother's plans. It could lead to a showdown that would reveal Amanda's darkest secret.

And so, against the backdrop of Gregory's words, Amanda thought intently about John Thorne. She released Gregory's hand and recalled the calloused roughness of John Thorne's workman's hands gripping her arms. John Thorne, who by possessing her had become her possession. And a taunt to the powers that had kept her a pampered prisoner. She thought long and hard about John Thorne, and reminded herself that in a game this dangerous, rules were made to be broken.

Gregory Forrest continued to endure Amanda's whims. But on that evening when he sat through the endless dinner without her, he was close to giving up. Amanda spent more and more time in her room, mildly indisposed. Gregory knew not to worry about her health. His worries were all centered on their future. He clenched his square hands beneath the table and longed, just for a moment, for the kind of woman he could bend to his will. But in arrogance he was no match for Amanda, and he knew it.

A door to the dining room, half hidden by a screen, opened silently, and a maid in a white cap bore in a tray of water ices in stemmed silver. As she passed the tray to the butler, Gregory noticed her. Only a glimpse and she was gone. For an instant it might have been Amanda herself. The same violet eyes in the serene, pale face. He wouldn't put it past Amanda to playact a servant's role at a dinner she'd refused to share with him.

Mary had seen him. He was as handsome as Miss Amanda had said: faraway eyes in a firmly set face. A god among barons and earls. The vision of him, and the sumptuous dining table, blinded her so that she nearly missed her footing. Midnight came before she could be alone with her thoughts, and then she was too tired to think. Though she was no stranger to hard work, Mary could barely stagger up all the flights to her little cell under the slope of the roof.

She fell on the narrow iron bed and was asleep at once, dreaming that she served the young American gentleman dining all alone at a great, glittering table.

Suddenly she sat bolt upright. She recognized none of the dark shapes in the room, and the dream had confused her. Thinking that she was dreaming still, she rose and moved to the door. Her dark hair hung loose, and her old nightgown billowed in the drafts. She moved along the passageway outside as if summoned by a distant voice, sleepwalking, if that was what it was. Her feet found the treacherous stairs, and she walked down them until she stepped into the deep luxury of a carpet.

She stood, coming to herself now, not a yard from Miss Amanda's door. Frightened, she was turning back toward the attic stairwell when a hand fell roughly on her shoulder.

I shall be murdered, Mary thought as the hand tightened. She was spun around and violently embraced. A man's hand caught both of hers in a vise behind her. His mouth sought hers, forcing her head back, roughly yet easily. She writhed against him, but one hard hand closed behind her neck, beneath her flowing hair.

Mary knew the clenching hand could kill her in a simple gesture. Instead, it found its way across her shoulders beneath the flimsy nightgown. A calloused hand, moving as confidently as if it had caressed her before.

The seam of Mary's gown tore from neck to shoulder.

She blinked back tears, too stunned for prayer, too frightened to call for help. "Please," she whispered. "I beg of you—don't."

"My God," he said. "Who are you?"

His hands fell away, and she was free now. In the darkness his head of pale, thick hair glowed dimly.

"I said, who are you?" he asked in a hoarse whisper.

"M-Miranda, sir—if you please."

"I know of no Miranda. Account for yourself before I—"

"I've only just come, sir. To be in service."

The man groaned. "Don't call me sir. I'm lower than you. Be off. Why in the devil are you roaming the halls at this hour? Did *she* ring for you?"

"No one sent for me. I—I—"

"Then forget this," he said, turning aside. Mary could almost make out his profile.

Her shaking hand found the stair rail. In the next second she'd vanished up to her attic. But John Thorne stood staring in the dark, stunned by what he'd done. Then he moved heavily along the hall, turned the noiseless knob he'd oiled himself, and strode into Amanda Whitwell's bedroom.

In the glow of the embers in the hearth he saw Amanda stir and stretch toward the lamp beside her bed. "Leave it dark, Amanda," he whispered, and reached out for her.

"My kidneys!" Mrs. Creeth whooped at Mr. Finley. "Treat yourself to a whiff of the aroma!"

Mr. Finley obliged by hovering over the steaming

pan. "I have said it before and I repeat it now. There is no one your equal in the matter of kidneys, Mrs. Creeth."

She glowed in triumph at the compliment she'd wrung out of the butler. It was only half past six, but Mrs. Creeth's kitchen was already halfway to breakfast. Porridge bubbled beside the matchless kidneys; bacon strips hung on hooks above the drip pan, ready to be thrust nearer the fire. Hilda and Hannah were giving the meager sum of their concentration to making toast.

Abel, the footman, was late as usual, for he walked over every morning from Bierley, taking his sweet time. "That Abel," Mrs. Creeth said, "will find no breakfast awaiting him in *these* kitchens." But Hilda, who would have thrown herself into the fire for one loving glance from Abel, slipped a slice of toast for him into her pocket.

In the apron room off the kitchen Betty Prowse, her mouth full of pins, was gathering the folds of a black uniform around Mary's form. If the previous night's terrifying encounter showed on Mary's face, Betty was too busy to notice. She took a tuck here and there until Mary's slim figure began to emerge.

Patches of dark showed beneath Betty's button eyes, and Mary wondered if her new friend was quite well. "Whose uniform was it?" Mary asked.

"Oh, this was Lottie's, the head parlormaid's. Left behind in her haste when she flounced orf to London to marry the landlord of a public house—"

"*Betty!* Get the new one into her uniform and report to me this instant!" Mrs. Creeth bellowed.

"Anyhow," Betty said, "whether you're Mary or Miranda, you're a welcome change from that Lottie." She gave Mary a quick shy smile before rushing to do the cook's bidding.

The servants' breakfast at Whitwell Hall was the finest meal Mary had ever known. Porridge, lumpless, with thick cream and a dusting of sugar. Toast with both marmalade and butter. And a platter of bacon and sausages. Mary wondered how the breakfast to be laid in the dining room above could surpass this feast.

Over the clinking of cutlery, Mr. Finley called out, "I trust you passed a comfortable night, Mrs. Buckle?"

"Fitful," Mrs. Buckle snapped from a chair by the hearth. She ate from a tray in icy solitude, for she wouldn't put her feet under a table where Mrs. Creeth presided. "And I must say," Mrs. Buckle went on, "this bacon is quite inedible."

"Throw it on the fire, then," Mrs. Creeth barked.

It required all hands to convey the family breakfast up to the sideboards of the great dining room, a palace of mirrors in the morning light. The board groaned with Mrs. Creeth's famous kidneys, an entire school of kippers, ranks of crisp sausages, pink beef awash in cream. And hanging in the room the scent of fresh coffee. Bustling with the rest of them, Mary wondered if coffee tasted as marvelous as its scent promised.

By half past eight Mr. Finley stood ready to serve. Beside him was Abel, arrived at last. When the great double doors opened, the female servants were sent scurrying to the serving pantry. But not before Mary saw that the first down to breakfast was the American gentleman. She had only a glimpse of the coat of muted tweeds pulled taut over his broad shoulders, and the blue-blackness of his hair.

"Oooo, they are such slugabeds!" said Betty. "And the ladies will be ringin' for breakfast up in their rooms. Orl except for Lady Eleanor. She's always down for breakfast. So we might as well pull down the trays from the shelf now, Mary."

A curious device hung on the wall of the servants' hall. It was a board with numbered squares matching all the rooms of the house. Whenever a button was touched in a chamber above, a bell chimed on the board, and a black card dropped into the square, summoning a servant. The contraption was Mr. Finley's greatest earthly joy. Betty referred to the board as Old Buzz-and-Jump.

The board chimed, announcing that Mrs. Glaslough had rung for her breakfast. "You, Mary—Miranda!" Mr. Finley called. "Take up Mrs. Glaslough's tray. And mind you knock and wait to be summoned. There's to be no bursting in on Mrs. Glaslough."

As Mary passed the foot of the attic stairs, she grew cold, remembering the night before. The odd confidences of the impulsive Miss Amanda, hinting of a man she could be flogged for loving. Then later, the dark encounter in the dead of night, the grip of the stranger's hands. Her heart pounded as she knocked at Mrs. Glaslough's door.

It was answered, and she entered with downcast eyes. She thought it was perhaps only her imagination that the door to Mrs. Glaslough's dressing room seemed to be just closing, as if someone had lingered until the last moment before leaving.

"Good morning, madam," Mary said quietly. "I hope you rested."

Mrs. Glaslough swept a fiery strand of hair from her

brow and looked intently at Mary. "As it happens, I had a somewhat *tempestuous* night, and I'm pining for my tea. Pour it out, won't you? No sugar."

When she had done so, Mary stooped to retrieve a pair of silk slippers from beneath the bed, and her eye was drawn to an empty champagne bottle lolling there.

"In the names of all the saints, don't open the curtains," Mrs. Glaslough said. "I abhor daylight—what I've seen of it." She divided a peach with a small silver knife. "This peach is just the least bit overripe—not unlike myself."

Making no sense of that observation, Mary started to withdraw, but Mrs. Glaslough said, "What is your name?"

"I'm called—Miranda, madam."

"I suppose you are quite used to hearing you are very like young Amanda—in appearance."

"Oh no, madam," Mary said. "I only began yesterday. But perhaps Miss Amanda did notice a similarity. She told me to take off my cap, and she looked at me."

"Yes, Miss Amanda *would* be attracted to any reflection of herself. I am one of Lady Eleanor's oldest friends, though rather earthy for her taste. You'll find her quite human beneath the grandeur. It's Amanda who wants watching. Do keep your guard up, Miranda. And now you may go."

When Old Buzz-and-Jump announced Amanda's desire for breakfast, Betty was sent up with her tray. But she was soon back, eyes brimming. "She sent me packin', she did," Betty announced to the kitchen. "Sez it's Miranda who's to fetch and carry for her from henceforth— her very words! Oooo, she's ever so high-handed this mornin', is Miss Amanda."

Miranda's eyes remained on the snowy linen of the tea towels she was folding. Mr. Finley, beside her, asserted his command. "We'll have to put up with Miss Amanda's anger, at least until the guests are gone and I can take up the matter with Lady Eleanor. Until then, Miranda will be occupied with tasks elsewhere in the house. Mrs. Buckle, I'm sure you can find a way to reassert your former authority over Miss Amanda."

Mrs. Buckle's face showed cautious satisfaction at this decision. And Miranda spent the rest of the day in duties that kept her well away from Amanda Whitwell's door. She was equal to the work, fitting neatly into the routine of the domestic staff. Even Mrs. Creeth could find little to complain of in her.

It was only when night drew on and Abel and Mr. Finley were laying the fires that Miranda felt a foreboding. With only twelve at dinner the house seemed nearly empty. That emptiness and the slow settling of darkness nagged at Miranda's heart. And she felt no better when she learned that the rooms where Betty and Mrs. Creeth and Mrs. Buckle slept were all in the attics of other wings of the house.

It was nearly bedtime before Betty and Hilda and Hannah returned from turning out the bedrooms of the departed guests. Betty bore aloft the champagne bottle from under Mrs. Glaslough's bed. "Oooo! That Mrs. Glaslough, she didn't polish orf orl that champagne by her lonesome."

From her place by the fire, Mrs. Creeth told Betty to mind her tongue.

But Betty flowed on. "And that American gent, Mr. Forrest, he's orf in the mornin' by the looks of things. But

I suppose he'll catch up wiv Miss Amanda again in November, when the family's in London."

"He's well out of it," Mrs. Creeth muttered.

"Here, stuff this in your pocket," Betty murmured, brushing past Miranda to slip an envelope into her hand.

Later, in the apron room with Betty peering over her shoulder, Miranda opened the envelope, and a pound note dropped out. "A pound?" She stared. "Twenty shillings?"

"Well, it's addressed to you, and I found it on Mrs. Glaslough's night table, so it's your tip. She must have taken a likin' to you," Betty mused.

And so Miranda entered finally into the ranks of the serving class, having received her first largesse from the casual and capricious hand of the mighty.

By the light of a flickering candle, Miranda found her attic room and shot a flimsy bolt behind her. The new electrical wiring didn't reach as high as the servants' quarters, and the candle's pale glow made hardly a dent in the darkness. But then the moon came out from a cloud and looked in at her through the slanting window. And some strange spell came over her.

It was partly the moonlight, and something more. A longing, perhaps, for the sea. Even as a child she'd yearned to stand and watch the waves break on the rocks. But there'd been no time for that luxury. She crept under the thin blanket, and her mind drifted in the moonlight. But then she was aware of someone she couldn't see.

Throwing back the blanket, she rose to her knees to the open window above her. When she stood on the bed, she was more than head and shoulders above the sill, and she lifted herself over it and onto the roof.

An arm's length in front of her was a parapet. She reached for it and anchored herself there to look down to a garden terraced and scalloped in degrees of darkness. She saw a lawn, flat as a ballroom floor, and before it a terrace balanced at intervals by empty stone urns.

In a scene as still as a painting, one of the urns changed its shape. Someone had been standing beside it and was moving on now—a shrouded figure, deeply bent, with black skirts fanning out behind and a shawl pulled over hunched shoulders. Only a white hand thrust from the shroud to grasp a cane. It was of some polished wood, like a crystal wand in the moonlight. Minutes passed as the figure crept slowly on in silence. Then the apparition was lost to view.

Miranda slid silently back through the window and shut it tight. In her bed she sought the escape of sleep. As her mind withdrew from the vision in the haunted garden, she sobbed once, giving way to fear of all the horrors that lay about her in the world.

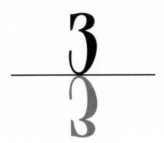

A bit of peace and quiet won't be unwelcome," Mrs. Creeth said to Miranda, almost friendly. The house party had continued to disband. "You're settling in, then, are you, my girl?"

"Yes, thank you, Mrs. Creeth."

Miranda longed to confide in her—or in some older woman—about the mysteries of Whitwell Hall. But Mrs. Creeth would bridle at even a cautious question. Miranda went on her way to tidy the morning room.

Betty had shown her the underground passage running from the kitchens to the front of the house. A flight at the far end rose to a nearly invisible door set in the paneling of the front hall. From there Miranda had only to cross the hall to reach the morning room.

She was through the invisible door before she saw the American gentleman there, with his back to her. His luggage was heaped beside the table. Miranda stopped dead, thinking of retreat. But she seemed rooted to the spot, her eyes following the line of his shoulders, then dropping to the heavy square hands clasped behind him. They were smooth and white. She'd never seen such hands, clasped easily, with strength held lightly in reserve. Not the work-hardened hands that had torn at her in the darkness. Not her assailant's.

Shivering, she ran a hand over her arm. The starchy sleeve rustled. Gregory Forrest turned, and their eyes met before she could look away. He smiled, and his smile was just the least bit crooked. Miranda smiled back, forgetting all her training.

"I think we've met before," he said, "or almost. In the dining room. You were working, and I was eating. That almost amounts to an introduction, doesn't it?"

"Oh, I shouldn't think so, sir," she said, finally lowering her eyes. She stood there until it dawned on her that he was waiting for her to introduce herself. A strange request.

"They call me Miranda, sir," she whispered, deeply embarrassed.

"How do you do, Miranda. I'm Gregory Forrest. And your last name?"

"Cooke, sir—but they don't call me that here." The outlandish idea that Mr. Forrest might call her Miss Cooke in the presence of others stunned her. Perhaps this was what Miss Amanda had against this otherwise perfect man. Not that he didn't know his place, but that he didn't know the place of others.

"You gave me quite a surprise the other night," he said. "I had the idea you were Amanda disguised as an honest working girl." Miranda wondered how often this supposed resemblance was to be remarked upon. "And in the cold light of day the resemblance is just as striking."

He seemed to know he was making matters awkward for her and changed his tack. "It's a very beautiful house. Especially Lady Eleanor's own sitting room, which I was honored to visit exactly once. Then I knew I was being taken seriously by at least one of the Whitwell ladies."

"I haven't seen Lady Eleanor's sitting room, sir."

"Well, you should," Mr. Forrest said. "I'll ask her to show it to you sometime. In fact, I could ask her now."

A soft footstep sounded on the grand staircase. It could only be Lady Eleanor. If she didn't move now, Miranda would be discovered chatting with Miss Amanda's fiancé. Gregory Forrest glanced toward the staircase, and when he turned back, expecting to see the beautiful hired girl so like a demure twin of Amanda, she was gone. The strangely supernatural effect of her vanishing act would baffle him for days.

With pounding heart, Miranda stood behind the invisible door, waiting there until Lady Eleanor and Mr. Forrest said their good-byes. Through the thin door she heard Lady Eleanor's voice, as sultry as its cultured rhythms allowed. "My dear Mr. Forrest—Gregory—we've let you down on this visit. Something is clearly troubling Amanda, and I'm afraid it's entirely like her to trouble others at such times. In another girl, it might be shyness, but in Amanda's case we both know better."

"I'm willing to wait, Lady Eleanor," Mr. Forrest said.

"Few men have your patience. I think you're right to return to London now. You have your studies, and to speak plainly, your presence may be prolonging Amanda's tiresomeness. But we shall see you when we come up to London in November."

Miranda heard the great double front doors open. "Here's Thorne now to collect your things," Lady Eleanor was saying. Then the flurry of good-byes, and finally the sound of silk subsiding into stillness.

Easing open the door in the paneling, Miranda hurried across to her duties in the morning room. Had she looked out a front window, she would have seen the two men who were both miserably in love with Amanda Whitwell. Gregory Forrest settling into the rear seat of Sir Timothy's shuddering new Lanchester motorcar, and John Thorne strapping the suitcases onto the running board.

Thorne swung himself up into the driver's seat, and the Lanchester lurched, then glided off between the Italian pines toward the distant gate.

In the days that followed, Hannah and Hilda gawped without envy at the amount of work Miranda could get through with a quiet efficiency. On the Friday evening of her first week, there was a mildly festive air around the table in the servants' hall. At the end of a hurried meal, Mr. Finley rose and withdrew a handful of brown envelopes from his breast pocket. He cleared his throat importantly. "For the benefit of one among us who has not yet learned our ways, I will just touch briefly upon the manner of financial—ah—remuneration traditional at Whitwell Hall. On the second Friday of every month wages are distributed. As you know . . ."

Mr. Finley flowed on until each in turn received

an envelope. Miranda was awed that in her first week she was worth thirty shillings, including Mrs. Glaslough's colossal tip.

But at that moment came a thunderous pounding at the door. "Who in the world at this hour?" Mrs. Creeth started in her chair. "See who it is, Hannah, but take care!"

Hannah's reluctant hand drew back the bolt. A familiar voice on the other side seemed to give her assurance. She pulled open the door, and a tide of wet leaves blew in, carried on a rain-laden night wind.

A boy of fourteen staggered inside. Miranda, fearful of the night that settled on this house, stared at him. The swinging lamps threw shadows across his white face. His eyes were enormous. He put down a storm lantern while Hannah threw her considerable weight against the door.

"It's that cheeky monkey, Willie Salter, the estate agent's son!" Mrs. Creeth said, on her feet now with hands planted on hips. "Frightening the wits out of us!"

"Speak up, boy!" Mr. Finley said. "What brings you here?"

"Why, he's wet through!" Mrs. Buckle said. "Come to the fire, Willie."

In a breaking voice he said, "I came up to the stables—the garages—for John Thorne. But I didn't find him. It's old Gran." His wet face began to crumple. "She's been set on and half strangled with a length of wire. It'll be the old madman's work—her own son. It'll be Bart Thorne. Oh, sir, Gran needs help bad!"

The butler reached the boy in two strides. "Are you babbling, Willie?"

"It's God's truth, Mr. Finley. I went down Smuggler's

Cottage way to see if John Thorne might let me look at his automobile books. The cottage door was half off its hinges, and inside, Granny Thorne was on the hearth rug. She—she—" Willie began to shake uncontrollably.

"Hannah!" Mr. Finley said, galvanized into action. "Set out with a storm lantern and find John Thorne! Send him on the run to the cottage."

"With the ole madman runnin' amok, Mr. Finley?" Hannah quaked.

"We know nothing for certain. But take Hilda with you, and a carving knife if it will give you courage!

"Mrs. Buckle," he said in a quieter tone. "Inform Her Ladyship that Granny Thorne is poorly and needs Dr. Post from Ventnor. We can only hope the wind hasn't taken the telephone line down." To Mrs. Creeth he said, "Get the wet things off that boy." And to Betty, "You are to make a circuit of the house, girl, securing the doors and windows. Then return to assist Mrs. Creeth in preparing some hot food to stand ready."

Betty stared, her active imagination running rampant among the horrors of a howling wind. She scuttled off, green with fear.

"And, Miranda." Mr. Finley turned to her. "You will accompany me to Granny Thorne's cottage, where you will be much needed. Have you the stomach for it, my girl?"

Miranda could only nod.

Now Miranda was stumbling behind Mr. Finley's bobbing lamp in a pair of borrowed boots and a streaming black rubber raincoat thrown over her head.

"It will be heavy going along the path around the mere," he shouted over the screaming wind. Past the outbuildings they crossed the rolled lawn, then rougher ground, and there ahead Miranda could see the thrashing darkness of a grove of trees. Lightning stabbed the sky as they made their way along the snaking path. It was another ten minutes' hard traveling before a yellow light in a clearing brought them to the cottage.

The shattered door hung by a hinge. This wasn't the work of the wind. A lamp in the middle of the room drew them inside. Finley shrugged out of his rubber coat. Miranda kept at his heels, her heart thumping.

An old woman sprawled on the hearth rug like a broken doll. Her head at an angle lay perilously near the glowing embers in the grate. Long strands of gray hair fell around her face, fanning out on the floor. A length of stout baling wire was looped around her neck. It had been loosened, undoubtedly by the boy, Willie, but it remained coiled above her wrinkled throat.

Mr. Finley dropped to one knee and took up a thin arm. At once the old woman drew a deep, shuddering breath. "She's alive," he said quietly, drawing the gleaming wire away from the fragile neck.

Miranda was certain she'd seen this old woman before. But now Mr. Finley said, "We must get the poor soul up to her bed." Miranda took the lantern and made for the narrow stairs that led up under the eaves.

"Miranda, perhaps I should have a look around upstairs first," Mr. Finley said. But there was nothing ominous in the two tiny rooms above. The one at the back belonging to John Thorne couldn't conceal a cat. The butler lit the wick of a lamp in Granny Thorne's bedroom, and soon she was resting in her own bed. Mr. Finley and Miranda kept watch from a pair of chairs on either side of the bed.

In the quiet, the butler chanced a bit of conversation. "She's near ninety. The story is that Granny's husband had been a smuggler before he came ashore and turned farmer. Very likely only folklore, but this place has always been called Smuggler's Cottage. The Thornes lived in this land long before Sir Timothy bought the estate in 1894. In the old days the place ran to a thousand acres and paid its way. The men worked the land and their women served in the Hall."

Caught up in memories, Finley grew expansive. "It was bitter for the tenants when most of the farms were sold off and the Hall became a country place for a gentleman in trade. The land they'd rented was up for sale and no money to buy it. There were some new opportunities—gardeners' work—but few people had the wit to grasp them. Granny Thorne's grandson, John, though, is of a new breed. Sees himself as a twentieth-century man, I shouldn't wonder."

Mr. Finley sniffed with disapproval. "Young Thorne's motor-mad. He's broken with the old ways, though I will say he's good to his old grandmother. But there's a streak of madness in this family." He paused and seemed to think better of saying more.

In the long silence Miranda realized the storm had abated. Mr. Finley dozed, and she slept soundly in the chair. A bird's trilling woke her in gray morning light. She hoped Mr. Finley hadn't noticed her asleep at her post. Then she saw the hand resting heavily on the coverlet beside the old woman's slight form. A powerful brown hand with grease-blackened fingernails. It was far from being Mr. Finley's.

Glancing up in fear, Miranda stared into the eyes of the man sitting where Mr. Finley had been. Daylight played across his craggy face and his tumble of blond hair. His shirtsleeves were rolled up, revealing forearms firmly muscled and covered with golden hair. It was John Thorne, impassively gazing at her with eyes the color of dawn.

She knew him in the first moment. And more. She'd been caught up in those thick arms, mauled by those hands. But she'd never seen the cool gray eyes or the set of the chin. She sat mesmerized. His was the kind of strength she'd always feared, though she'd suffered at no other man's hands but his.

At last, she looked aside. In the far corner of the room, leaning against the wall, was the old woman's walking stick, a shiny black malacca cane. Like a puzzle piece falling into place, the cane seemed to complete Miranda's understanding about these people. The cane told her the apparition she'd seen in the moonlit garden had been Granny Thorne. And her grandson was the man who'd assailed Miranda with such confident familiarity on that first night. These two creatures of darkness were ordinary mortals after all. Miranda wondered why her fear of them didn't ebb at once.

Hilda and Hannah had encountered John Thorne on the home farm path. Their hysteria and the brandished carving knife, their gasped "madman" and "Granny Thorne," had sent him on the run to Smuggler's Cottage. If a maniac from the Newport lunatic asylum was loose on the grounds, he knew well who it was. But he couldn't have known how near he'd come to him. For under a slab of rock beside the mere, the madman—his father, Bart Thorne—was lying, covered in slime.

The madman's disordered mind had registered the sound of footsteps on the path: the headlong stumbling of the two kitchen maids, the heavy footfalls of John Thorne. Bart lay as still as death until the sounds were lost in the moaning wind.

It was in the darkest part of night when John Thorne found Finley and the slumbering Miranda at his grandmother's bedside. He and the butler murmured together, Finley saying, "The Ventnor police, Thorne. We had better get through to them."

"What's the point?" John muttered back. "He'd make straight for this place and nowhere else. His mind's ruled by this plot of earth. He'll keep coming back as long as he's able. And he knows every twig and turning. I'm the only one who could track him down."

"The family," Finley said, working his hands in anguish. "Sir Timothy and Lady Eleanor. We must not disturb the family with this terrible business."

The butler hurried back to the Hall while John Thorne sat down to keep watch. Granny would survive this, he hoped, for she'd survived much else. And he spared a thought for his father as well. He longed to see the old maniac under lock and key again—safe from a world he could no longer live in.

Thorne's eye drifted across to Miranda and lingered. He'd cursed himself for a week for accosting this girl outside Amanda's door. Indeed, if he'd inherited any insanity from his family, he decided it had surfaced the day

Amanda Whitwell had beclouded his brain. She'd held him in her grasp from the first moment he'd locked her in his arms, though they could have no future together. He feared in his heart that Amanda was claiming his soul. John Thorne returned with relief to contemplate the girl across from him, the girl who could be Amanda's double, but hardly her match.

He found himself keeping watch over her sleeping form. His eye followed the shadowed line of her temple, the damp ringlets that had escaped the severe restraint of her cap. Something stirred in him and yearned toward her—only her. He jerked himself back from such idiocy. To be inflamed by one woman—so unattainable and so available—and to be drawn to another might be proof of madness outright.

John Thorne had been born in this bed. His mother had died giving him life some twelve years before the estate was divided and the earth shifted beneath his family's feet.

If his raising had been left to Granny Thorne, he might have roamed these fields at will. But his bull-necked father recognized none of the rights of boyhood. Embittered at the loss of his wife, who'd died to replace her useful self with this lawless brat, Bart Thorne had turned himself into a beast of burden. The land he worked became his obsession, and he came to believe it belonged to him. He had only contempt for his own mother, Granny Thorne, who took an innocent pleasure in sometimes "helping out" up at the Hall.

John Thorne's first memories were of the sky-blue days when he'd scaled the tallest tree in the grove. Its topmost branch became his conning tower. From this swaying perch sixty feet above ground he could survey Whitwell Hall, the roofs of Ventnor, and the green-gold sea stretching away to the hazy horizon. His dreams took him across the Atlantic in Spanish galleons, sleek liners, even balloons. There at the top of the tree, John fell in love with freedom.

But the moment was shattered by his father's enraged roar when he saw his only potential unpaid farmhand hanging between life and death on a branch far above.

The thundering voice brought the boy scrambling down, leaving half his skin on the rough bark. Bart Thorne flayed John further, without mercy. He said little at the best of times. In anger, a leather strap spoke for him.

That was the last day of John's boyhood. Harnessed in tandem with the plow horse, he followed the furrows as the disc turned the unyielding soil. The marginal land had never produced quite enough. In many a lean winter the only money the household saw was what Granny's sewing and mending at the Hall brought in. Every penny of this meager sum became a taunt to Bart Thorne's darkening mind.

John came to see his father as a man clinging to the final shreds of an unworkable way of life. A man without imagination who stood frozen between two generations—a salty, long-dead smuggler and a young son who would chart an unknown course.

Bart Thorne spiraled downward—days befuddled by brute labor, nights by drink. He took to sleeping in the barn like an animal. On the night John turned seventeen, his father set fire to a small outbuilding. The flames threw mad shadows into the grove. John found Bart standing beyond the ring of firelight, mouth slavering.

Sir Timothy as new master at the Hall sent for the asylum authorities, and Granny signed the papers for her son's committal.

But now he was back to attack the old woman at her own hearthside.

The blond and bronzed man sitting across from her seemed lost in thought. But his eyes were upon her, bidding her to speak. At last she said, "I shouldn't have slept."

"Even the voice is the same," John Thorne muttered. "Do you know me?"

"I know you," she said quietly. "They call me—"

"I know what they call you. As soon as someone comes to sit with Gran, I'll see you safely back."

"I'd sooner go now," Miranda said, stirring.

"I'd sooner you didn't." And so they sat, Miranda trapped a second time by the will of this man.

Granny Thorne opened her eyes and turned toward Miranda. "Why, Miss Amanda, you oughtn't to have troubled yourself."

"It's not Miss Amanda, Granny," Thorne said sharply. "It's a maid from the Hall."

"John?" She turned toward him. "Oh, John, he's back. Whatever shall we do?"

Her withered hand closed around John's wrist. "He didn't know me, John. Not properly. He took me for a wicked spirit that had stolen his land. Then with a nasty bit of wire he—" She gave way to weeping, drawing her grandson closer to hide her face in his shoulder.

He was gentle with the old woman, Miranda noticed. She thought he'd been right to let her talk. Thorne returned his gaze to Miranda, who met it with a feeling of sympathy shared.

In another moment, the room filled with intruders. Dr. Post, looking brisk and put-upon, swung his black bag on the bed and looked inquiringly at John Thorne. Then Mrs. Creeth bore in a cloth-covered basket, followed by a towering, moonfaced man. It was George Salter, father of Willie and estate agent for the Whitwells.

"Well now, old woman," the doctor said to Granny Thorne, "I see the reports of your death are much magnified. What is it? Have you taken one of your turns?"

"Turns! I don't *have* turns, as you'd know if you were a proper doctor."

That startled Miranda, but then she saw there was an old bond between these two.

"Let's have a look at you anyway." Dr. Post found the angry red line encircling her throat. "Good Lord! Will somebody tell me what's going on around here?"

"Send out the rest and I'll put you in the picture, Dr. Post," Granny piped from her bed.

"Not a bad idea, though it does come from you, Granny," he said, and sent the others off down the stairs. Mrs. Creeth ordered Miranda back to the kitchens, then looked dubious when she saw that John Thorne meant to see her safely there. Her gaze followed the young people out of the cottage.

The path through the grove was narrow, and Miranda's sleeve brushed John's. With the sun up, it was a morning to remind her of the day she'd met the Wisewoman. A day as warm as this one promised to be, with the hint of autumn ahead. In the pleasure of this temporary freedom, she almost forgot to fear her companion.

As they neared the misty waters of the mere, John said, "It's my old dad causing all this, if you haven't guessed. He's the madman that set on Granny—his own mother. The land drove him to it. I was just seventeen when they had to lock him away. And I was off to the wars the next day. South Africa. I knew I'd find no discipline in the whole of the British Army to rival my dad's."

Now they'd come to the mere, lying like a vast saucer beside the path. On the far shore near a great rock where two paths diverged was a kind of Grecian temple. A tight circle of columns supported a stone dome.

Miranda lingered, caught up in the serene beauty of the circular mere and the perfect temple rising above it. This rain-washed vista made her heart yearn and sing.

"It's called a folly," John Thorne said. "That temple thing. A folly, I suppose, because it serves no purpose."

She turned from his side, the moment shattered, and set a brisk pace toward the house.

He caught up, sensing something had gone wrong and wondering why it mattered to him. It could only be her resemblance to Amanda that drew him. She was a servant, and he'd had his full share of servant girls before he'd fallen into Amanda's web. Still, he tried to think of something to appease her.

"You'll be all right now," he said at last when they reached the outbuildings. "He'll be caught, my dad—"

Miranda turned and looked suddenly up at him. "Why did you come back? After the war. Why did you come back to this place?" There was a challenge in the bold question.

"I—I suppose it was my fate. I had a hundred plans, but when I was free, I came straight back. I guess it was my fate."

And mine, Miranda thought, wondering if she herself was going slightly mad.

When Miranda had closed the kitchen door against John Thorne, she felt close to fainting with fatigue and with another emotion, harder to recognize. The kitchen was quiet, but descending the stairs from the dining room were Mrs. Buckle and Mr. Finley, deep in conversation.

"I left Her Ladyship with the impression that the old woman had taken sick," Mrs. Buckle was saying.

"And you were quite right," the butler said. "For the present, I wish to spare the family the knowledge that old Thorne is back and very likely still within the grounds. It's unfair that they should have visited upon them this— creature—of a past for which they have no responsibility."

"Ah, Mr. Finley," the housekeeper declared, "when the family acquired this property, they little reckoned on the legacy of . . . depravity they fell heir to."

Mr. Finley nearly leaped to see Miranda there within hearing of their privileged conversation. "Miranda, at last! You have not done badly in these past hours, and you have shown your mettle. But unfortunately, Betty appears to be slacking her duties. You must see to her, and if there is nothing seriously wrong, you are to rout her out at once."

Mrs. Buckle directed Miranda to Betty's rooms, high in the house. As Miranda negotiated all the flights and turnings, it was as if John Thorne's gray eyes still followed her. She knew he wasn't trusted among the servants. Perhaps it was his coarseness. Or the madness that stalked his family. But it was more likely John Thorne's arrogant independence that vexed them all.

It was only a show, Miranda decided, for what freedom did he possess? Then she thought of the gentle regret in his voice when he'd told her of his mad father. Nothing fitted about this John Thorne. And perhaps that was the greatest cause of his unpopularity.

Near Betty's door, a sharp, sour smell cut the mustiness of the attics. Betty lay across a disorderly bed, where she'd been very sick. Miranda dipped a towel into a pitcher of water and set about tidying up the girl.

"What is it, Betty? The doctor is with Granny Thorne now. Shall I ask Mr. Finley to send for him?"

"Wot? A doctor? He can't prescribe nuffin for wot I got."

"What have you got, Betty?" Miranda asked.

"Wot I've got is a little stranger comin'," Betty muttered.

"A baby, Betty? You?"

"That's right." Betty sighed. "A baby and me."

The night's storm had kept her wakeful and tossing, and Amanda Whitwell was up at first light. She flung out of her bed and pulled her billowing nightgown around herself, drawing it in tightly at her narrow waist. Unquestionably, she'd taken off a few pounds.

Amanda kept watch over her weight, for the new fashions called for wasplike waists and a swanlike line from bosom to hip. The day of the well-nourished English beauty had passed. Out with great lumps of girls like her friend Sybil Ward-Benedict, that monument to a robust appetite. Poor Sybil, Amanda thought. How unfashionable her ample thigh and jutting prow have grown to be.

Amanda crossed the room to fix a rattling window. The windows were set in a great three-sided bay of carved stone that reminded her somehow of the bridge of an ocean liner. No matter that her ship seemed to have gone aground in a garden. And no matter that the only water in view was the mere. But instead of latching the window against the morning breeze, she pushed it open. Mist rose from the mere against the stone temple on the other shore. It struck Amanda as an ideal day for a walk.

She turned to select something tweedy, then remembered her resolve not to leave her room until she had secured Miranda as her own maid instead of the beastly Buckle. Her mother was being tiresome about the new girl, claiming she needed more training. Amanda's patience was drawing to an end. I shall have Miranda before the week is out or else, she thought. And I shall have that walk in any case.

Amanda decided on a full Sybil Ward-Benedict breakfast, from kippers to scones, and rang for Buckle. She'd turned away from the window just as John Thorne and Miranda stepped out together from the grove. Amanda would have forgotten her breakfast plans had she seen them, brushing against one another, lingering to look out across the mere. Amanda would have thrown the tantrum of all tantrums. But she saw nothing, for Mrs. Buckle entered with the usual morning tea tray.

Not noticing that the woman was distracted, Amanda said, "Oh, Buckle, I'm famished! Have a bit of everything from the sideboard sent up."

Mrs. Buckle blinked at this change of tack.

"And, Buckle, if we must go up to London in November, I shall need new clothes. But oughtn't we to salvage some of my older things as well?"

"Indeed, miss," the housekeeper said with lowered eyes.

"I might get another wearing out of this gray crepe, but just see where the lining has pulled away. A job for Granny Thorne. Here, take it to her."

"Oh, Miss Amanda, I don't think—"

"*Do* take it, and see that Granny gets it."

After a hearty breakfast Amanda pulled a tweed coat and skirt from her wardrobe, and a small three-cornered hat. Soon now she'd have a proper maid to lay out her clothes. With a wool scarf wound around her neck, she crept with exaggerated care past her mother's door. She left the house through a long window in the morning room because that was how John Thorne entered when he came to her by night.

Amanda ran down the terrace steps and across the lawn, making for the mere. Circling it in her squishing shoes, she sat on the great stone slab near the temple and recalled that here, last June in Coronation Week, John Thorne had first made love to her.

Rising, she walked past the temple along a broad

green sweep between top-heavy rhododendrons. At the end was a round garden, almost hidden, where she'd played as a child. The end of the world, it had seemed to her then. In the secluded garden stood a ring of stone monuments carved as griffins, leopards, tigers. Lingering in the center of the circle, she recalled a childhood lonelier than it had needed to be because of her difficult ways.

Behind her a stone leopard seemed to move—so silently that Amanda sensed nothing. The leopard kept to its plinth, but from behind it Bart Thorne stepped.

He'd crouched all night beneath the rock at the mere's edge and had crept all morning among the rhododendrons. He'd known a moment of clarity toward dawn, realizing he was back on his own land again. But now he was confused. The patchwork of his farmed land had vanished, his fields overgrown, his fences unmended.

Bart Thorne saw his land was under an evil spell. Even the woman who sat in his mother's place by the cottage fire was a witch. This crone had used her unspeakable powers to rob him of everything.

Bart Thorne began to move forward. He was standing behind Amanda before she felt his presence. To him she was some young hussy, giving herself airs on his hard-won acres. His knobby hands closed over the ends of her wool scarf.

Amanda's head jerked suddenly back. She screamed soundlessly as the scarf cut off her breath. She felt nothing but surprise until the day turned black.

Amanda drifted between nightmare and nothingness. At times all the stone creatures came alive, lunging at one another in an epic battle. At other times she was drowsing in her bed. Whispered voices came and went. At still other times she cried out in panic. Then cool cloths were pressed to her forehead.

It was evening when she awoke. On one side of the bed sat her mother, and on the other side Miranda, very proper in a white wisp of a cap and no apron. Very much like a lady's maid. John Thorne stood at the foot of the bed, cap in hand. His unruly hair was burnished by lamplight. The scene shifted again and Sir Timothy was there beside her. Then someone was urging a curved straw between her lips. It was Buckle.

The London newspapers broke the story of the attack on Amanda Whitwell on an otherwise unremarkable Monday morning in September 1911:

KNIGHT'S BEAUTIFUL DAUGHTER
ESCAPES DEATH AT LUNATIC'S HAND

Amanda, daughter of Sir Timothy and Lady Eleanor Whitwell of Charles Street, London, and Whitwell Hall, Isle of Wight, was set upon last Saturday by an escaped inmate of St. Luke's Asylum in Newport. Miss Whitwell, taking a solitary stroll in the grounds of Whitwell Hall, was surprised by the man, identified as Bart Thorne. He had all but strangled Miss Whitwell with her own woolen scarf when her rescuer interrupted the assault.

The hero was John Thorne, the son of the attacker and a retainer of the Whitwell family, who was searching the grounds for his father at the time. The two men struggled over the unconscious Miss Whitwell, the lunatic turning his attack on his own son. At length the elder Thorne suffered an apparent

heart attack, staggered into a shallow lake, and fell dead. A
forthcoming inquest is expected to return no verdict against
John Thorne, who was forced to defend his master's daughter.

It has been learned that Miss Whitwell is suffering severely
from shock and has not fully regained consciousness.

One afternoon when Amanda awoke, her mind was utterly clear, and she sat bolt upright. She very nearly threw her legs over the side of the bed before she saw Gregory Forrest sitting there.

"My darling," Gregory said, reaching for her.

To forestall his embrace, Amanda took his hand. "Oh, Gregory," she said in annoyance, "I must have overslept."

At that he grinned. "It's my own Amanda, restored in spirit."

"Account for all this, Gregory! Whatever are you doing unchaperoned in my bedroom? I'm in an awful muddle, and I've had the most extraordinary dreams. Gregory, how long have I been drifting in this bed?"

"A week. Ten days."

"Good Lord! Then I've been ill. I remember . . ."

"Yes? What, darling?"

"I remember . . . the sculpture garden. It was lovely there. Then something very strange happened. Something—" Amanda tightened her grasp on his hand.

Then Gregory told Amanda the story of Bart Thorne—of whom she'd known nothing—as it had been pieced together by his son, by Finley, and by the authorities. She lay very still against the pillows, listening.

"Then John killed his own father to save me," she said.

"The man was old and sick, Amanda. As a result of the fight, he had a seizure and died. You're not to think you had any responsibility."

"John saved my life," Amanda said, as if she were in the room alone. But then she turned to Gregory and smiled. "Gregory, it took this to bring me to my senses. I've been foolish and willful, and I've made you miserable."

"Amanda, don't. It's enough for me to see you well again."

"You sat with me when I was unconscious?"

"Yes. There was always someone with you. You looked like Sleeping Beauty waiting for her kiss."

"You may give it to me now." But Gregory Forrest was already out of his chair and enfolding her in his arms. She returned his kisses with abandon. Her eyes shut, she thought of John Thorne and tightened her grasp on Gregory's shoulders. Even then she wondered how long the news of her recovery would take to reach Smuggler's Cottage.

"I owe a great debt to Thorne," she said when Gregory released her. "I must thank him. Perhaps a note. Bring me my writing materials, will you?"

While Gregory rummaged in the desk, Amanda ran a hand through her tangled hair. She must look a fright. If Gregory found her desirable at this moment, then love was blind indeed. In Gregory's case, she decided, it might have to be a great deal more blind in the future, and deaf. For there was no doubt in Amanda's mind that Thorne's sacrifice of his own father had bound them together in some final way. Up till now, Gregory had been only an inconvenience. That was over. Now he'd be very convenient indeed. Her last doubts fell away. From now on she would use every device—and everybody—to have John Thorne.

When she'd finished her note, she handed it to Gregory. "Be an angel and deliver this to Thorne yourself. Servants are so unreliable."

The note inside the sealed envelope was to the point:

John,
Come to me tonight.
A.

My mother taught me to serve but not to survive. And so I was less prepared to be a servant than she foresaw. I came to Whitwell Hall expecting to remain there all my life. I needed to succeed, for I had no home to go back to if I failed. I remained seven months.

Later, I had reason to remember my first day and my strange encounter with the Wisewoman. She spoke of husbands and marriages, death and rebirth, and if it hadn't been for the coin she gave me—an American Indianhead penny—I might have forgotten her words. But I carried it with me as something of my own. Even after I put on the quiet gray frock of Miss Amanda Whitwell's lady's maid, the coin was forever somewhere on my person.

As I think back, my life at Whitwell Hall truly began on that Saturday morning when I answered a thumping at the yard door. John Thorne stood there, cradling Miss

Amanda in his arms. He thrust her at me, and I staggered, for she was as heavy as I. Then he was gone, but I saw the marks on Miss Amanda's neck and knew the madman had struck again.

Mrs. Buckle and I carried her to her room and called Lady Eleanor. John Thorne returned to the mere and brought his father's body to shore. The drive filled with policemen, and the household was caught up in chaos. It was then that Her Ladyship told me I was to be Miss Amanda's own maid, and my duties began while she still lay quiet in her bed.

I had my work cut out for me just putting her wardrobe to rights. She had enough clothes for a whole village of young women, and I had many an excuse to bring Granny Thorne a basket of mending or a hem to turn. She always greeted me warmly and was as sane as her son was mad. She was resigned to his death, saying his mind had long since died. I found myself listening for any mention she might make of her grandson. But John Thorne never arose in her conversation.

Visitors gathered at Miss Amanda's bedside in those early days. Miss Ward-Benedict came at once, and stayed on, but the visitor who interested me most was Mr. Gregory Forrest. He was there within hours of reading the newspaper account, and it was hard work to persuade him to leave her, even for meals.

I suppose I had been in love with Gregory Forrest from the day I encountered him in the front hall. But it was an idolizing love, distant and make-believe, because of the difference in our stations in life. He spoke to me with great kindness. I attributed this to my resemblance to Miss Amanda, which clearly interested him, though it unnerved me severely. For all his kindness, he remained in my mind a storybook figure. I couldn't believe Miss Amanda didn't love him.

To my surprise, Mr. Finley granted me a half day off at the end of my first week, as a reward for my services. Betty was to have a half day as well, to keep me company, and I dreaded an afternoon with her. In my innocence, I thought she'd be desperate about her future and the future of her child. Clearly, her days at Whitwell Hall were numbered.

But when we met to go out, she was all smiles. She wore a decent coat and an extraordinary hat, its brim up in front and skewered with a peacock feather. We set off down the road to Ventnor. "We'll skate round the shops and take our tea at the hotel," she said. "Did you bring money?" I'd brought twenty of my thirty shillings, and suddenly my heart was singing with freedom.

I'd have lingered before every shop window in Ventnor, but Betty only slowed our pace outside Sampson & Son, Drapers. We tarried at the window until a tall, very pale man well past his first youth stepped out. His dark suit hung on his gangling frame, and he appeared to be lathering his hands with imaginary soap.

Clearly, Betty knew him. He addressed her with nervous excitement as "Miss Prowse," and I saw then we'd been heading for Sampson & Son, Drapers all along.

Betty introduced us. He was Hubert Sampson, the son of the long-deceased founder. Presently he escorted us through the shop and up a flight of stairs to a small cluttered parlor above. Before the fire sat an enormous woman who looked up in annoyance.

"Mother!" Mr. Sampson boomed. "Just see who I noticed passing the shop!"

She could hardly favor us with a look while Mr. Sampson tried gamely to cover her coldness with his own geniality. "Surely you'll both stop for tea with us," he said.

At that Mrs. Sampson said, "It's too early by far for tea, Hubert. I won't have the maid hurried." She gave Betty a look meant to remind her that she was a servant herself.

Mr. Sampson seemed to wither, but there was defiance in his eye, for he was taken with Betty. I thought the old woman clinging to her bachelor son might be going about it all the wrong way.

I had no experience of the sort of scheming Betty was up to. I never once thought Mr. Sampson was the father of her unborn child. He was nobody's idea of a seducer, and I was sure he knew nothing about the child. Yet I hoped that he would marry Betty despite everything—and soon.

When we rose to leave, some time after we should have, I had little desire for tea, but Betty dragged me along to the hotel. A waiter as icy as Mr. Finley himself bowed us to a table. And before the bread and butter and tea could be brought, Betty began again to bubble. "Of course, Miranda, he's miles above me and the . . . circumstances is difficult. But I think he fancies me, don't you? It's orful I'm not better spoken. But I was brought up in the orphanage. And he's ever such a gentleman. I don't know wot he sees in me, but I do need him." Betty struggled with herself, and her eyes glistened.

After tea we made our way back as slowly as we dared. The last shop in the town was a photographer's studio, where we lingered at the window, looking at the pictures of brides.

Then Betty was plucking my sleeve, and somehow we were inside the place. Before I knew it, she'd driven a bargain with the photographer, and we had our picture made for a shilling. In the photograph, Betty's hat dominates everything. Neither of us thought to smile, and I stare out upon the world with Miss Amanda's eyes. When I found the picture after many years, I was again unable to smile. I wept instead.

We were nearly back at the Hall before Betty said, "Mr. Sampson—Hubert's not the father-to-be. It was one of the cowboys from the Wild West Show this summer at Ventnor, though he wasn't a real one. Only a Cornishman who could ride. I slipped out night after night to meet him. I slipped out once too often, if the truth be told."

We reached the gates of Whitwell Hall with Betty's future hanging in the balance.

Later I was to wonder how early in our time together Miss Amanda had conceived the plan for my future, and her own. When I brought up her breakfast each morning, her eyes glittered thoughtfully at me. But I attributed this to the plans she had for filling my days with duties, and occupying my half days as well.

She changed her clothes three times a day and left her former attire scattered about the room. Miss Ward-Benedict, during her stay, was often underfoot too, and so my duties were complicated by two young ladies who sat gossiping and learning to smoke cigarettes while I endeavored to make ready my mistress's next outfit.

There was little real sympathy between Miss Amanda

and her friend, whose concerns were horses and racing meets. Miss Ward-Benedict was soon off, followed by Mr. Forrest, who was persuaded back to his studies in London.

I was expected to attend to my young lady and then to serve in the dining room under Mr. Finley. It was two jobs, but I enjoyed being in touch with the servants' hall. The talk there by mid-October was all about the fox-hunting season. I knew nothing of foxes, and I was much surprised at the enthusiasm Miss Amanda showed. I must have supposed that Miss Ward-Benedict's talk of hunting had given her a new interest. It dawned on me only later that she had quite a different reason.

On the night before the hunt she sent me in search of her walking boots and outdoor clothes. Then she said, "But, Miranda, we haven't thought what *you* will wear."

"I, Miss Amanda?" I had no idea that I'd be attending her at a fox hunt, but she began digging through the cupboards herself. In time she assembled a mustard-yellow jumper, a heather tweed coat and skirt, boots, and a hat. Then, when she'd had me put them on, she drew me over to a looking glass. We were both startled. In her clothes, I was Miss Amanda's double. She caught her breath and gazed at me, until I turned away.

On the day of the hunt we gathered on the front steps of the Hall to wait for the motorcars. Of a hunt I knew only that some rode horses and others followed on foot. Lady Eleanor wore a russet wool outfit that was hardly practical enough for anything more than standing in a dry porch.

Shortly a small motorcar driven by Mr. George Salter, the estate agent, drew up and Sir Timothy climbed in.

Then came the Lanchester with John Thorne at the wheel. Thorne stepped down from the driver's seat to hand Lady Eleanor and Miss Amanda up into the rear seat.

The automobile seemed immense to me as it throbbed all over to the rhythm of the engine. I stood rooted to the spot until Miss Amanda leaned down and called, "Come along, Miranda! You're to go up front with . . . Thorne." I hitched my skirts and feared for my life and climbed up.

John Thorne, his cap pulled down to his eyes, gave me only a sidelong glance and perhaps a bit of a smile at my nervousness as we rolled forward behind Mr. Salter. But I was soon carried away by the adventure and the sensation of speed. At last we drew near where the hunt was assembling.

Miss Amanda slipped down from the automobile before John Thorne could come around to assist her. She was to join a group of young people to follow the hunt on foot until the going got rough, then finish the day with a claret cup at one of the great houses in the neighborhood.

"Now, Miranda," she said, "Mother expects to join Lady Orton in a picnic lunch. And I shall not need you at all. You're to go with Thorne, who will explain—whatever there is to explain about the hunt. Won't you, Thorne? And then you can call for me in the motor when it's over."

"Yes, miss," John Thorne said, giving her a very direct look. Then he took my elbow in a familiar way and led me off, saying, "The great thing at a hunt is to have the drink they offer first."

Taking mugs of ale from trays nearby, we edged through the mob toward the hounds, which were straining at their leads, a great choppy mass of wagging tails and howling mouths and steaming breaths.

When the hounds heard the huntsman's horn, they surged off, suddenly free. I'd have been trampled by the oncoming horses if John Thorne hadn't drawn me aside. We waited while the horses and the foot followers had cleared the stone wall. Then he half lifted me over it, and we made off across the field after the others.

Instead of a mad dash, it was all leisurely with more wait than hurry-up. The fine horses cavorted and stamped in the distance while the horsewomen arranged and rearranged their skirts. The hounds grouped and regrouped, darted away and returned. The horsemen reined up behind them. Those on foot stood around in groups. Some, seeing a dry patch, sprawled about on the ground. My heart sang with the beauty of it.

There was a need growing within me to grasp at such moments as these. I'd been raised to expect nothing for myself. Yet expectation was rising in me.

Then suddenly we were running. The hounds had set off through a thicket with a purposeful cry. On the far side was pastureland. As John and I pounded across the field, his hand slipped down my arm to grasp my hand, and I could feel the warmth of it.

In the next cover I thought we were sure to find a nest of foxes. But if they'd been near before, they were farther off now. The day sped along in bursts of excitement until John and I sat down to rest inside the gate of a small stone church. We dropped down upon one of the ancient tombs that stood like a great marble table. I stole a glance at him. His profile was very fine, I thought. Strong and with the jutting chin of a quiet man. I seemed to grow at ease beside him until he broke the silence abruptly. "You're settling in up at the Hall?"

"I am that," I said.

"They've made you the young miss's own lady's maid?"

"They have."

"And how do you like her, then?"

"It's not for me to say, I'm sure," I said, primly.

He fixed me with eyes the color of the overcast sky. "Come now, Miranda, you must bend a bit or you'll be broken by the gale." The autumn leaves swirled across the graves as if to prove his warning.

I gazed at John Thorne, trying to see into him. Was there poetry and sentiment in his heart, or merely cynicism? Why was he not exactly what he was, like the rest of the servants?

"Why is it," he said, "when such as we can get away from our work for a rare bit of peace and quiet, we can think of nothing to talk of but our betters?"

"What else have we?" I asked, truly wanting to know.

"Only what we can take."

A distant huntsman's horn sounded a long blast and then another. "Gone to ground," John said. "The foxes have got clean away. I'm glad when they do. It sets the day in a proper perspective."

He rose then and offered me both his hands. Then he kissed me lightly on the cheek. It took me by surprise, the suddenness and the gentleness. We strolled off then, arm and arm, as if something had been decided between us.

Miss Amanda seemed to know before I did that John Thorne and I were courting in a quiet way. Before, it had seemed sensible to spend my life in service, keeping to myself. Now it seemed just as sensible to enjoy the company of a man who attracted me strongly. I was drawn to John half against my will. But that only added what Betty might call a bit of spice. And so I went about a trifle weak in the knees.

It's said that young girls are transformed by love. It was to be so with me, though not in the usual way. Without quite noticing it myself, I began to copy Miss Amanda's ways. Those that I admired, at any rate. The rough edges from my country speech fell away. I simply watched and listened to Miss Amanda and began to be a part of her. After all, she had Gregory Forrest eating from her hand, and that gave me an idea or two of my own.

I see now that Miss Amanda was too obliging by half. She'd dressed me in her clothes for the hunt, and from then on she seemed more and more determined to turn me into a mirror of herself, passing along quite new clothes she'd hardly worn. It was impossible to refuse them.

We began preparing for the London month, which was nearly upon us. A dressmaker from Ventnor, Miss Semple, came every day to see to the fittings for both Lady Eleanor and Miss Amanda. But soon Miss Amanda grew impatient, and I became her stand-in.

Miss Semple, bristling with pins, talked long about "ball gowns for galas." And when she gossiped about the annual tradesmen's dance and supper party to be held soon in Ventnor, it gave me an idea. "Are you making a ball gown for Mrs. Sampson? Hubert Sampson's mother?"

"Well, as you ask, no. Mrs. Sampson's dancing days are over."

Betty was more woebegone than ever. On her half days she'd linger outside Sampson & Son, Drapers. But not since the day we'd gone there together had Hubert Sampson acknowledged her presence. Betty was inclined to think that Hubert's mother had talked him out of seeing her. I was inclined to agree.

I was so preoccupied with Betty that when Miss Amanda demanded to know what was on my mind, I blurted it out. Miss Amanda showed the liveliest interest in Betty's case, and between us, we devised a plan.

Every year Sir Timothy bought a pair of tickets to the Ventnor Tradesmen's Ball and passed them along to the estate agent, Mr. Salter, and his sister, Winifred. Miss Amanda was to ask her father for another pair of tickets, while I was to get Mr. Sampson to the ball, where Betty would be waiting, as alluring as Miss Amanda and I could make her.

I was soon armed with the tickets, and on a half day Miss Amanda granted me for the purpose, I went to Sampson & Son, Drapers. Hubert remembered me and asked me up to see his mother. She already knew that I was Miss Amanda's own maid. Clearly, Miss Semple was a bearer of tales.

Murmuring that Miss Whitwell had given me two tickets to the ball, I asked Mrs. Sampson's advice regarding the propriety of the event. Her eyes narrowed. She saw my position at the Hall as somewhat exalted, nearer the gentry than she was herself, in a manner of speaking. Assuring me that only the best people went to the ball, she said, "Perhaps you'll allow my son to take you in. You'll have to find your own way there. But I daresay Hubert could give you his arm for the first set and into the supper room."

Hubert Sampson beamed like a much younger man. And his mother was beaming too, or near enough. She'd managed to dispel Betty by means of me. And her look clearly said that she'd deal with me later, if need be. Each of us was suffused with a different triumph, and I was urged to stay for tea.

Later Miss Amanda advanced the plan by her own scheming. "Of course, Betty will need a suitable frock," she said. "But what will you wear, Miranda?"

After deliberation, it was decided that I was to have a new dress, made by Miss Semple. White, with bands of purple velvet to outline a deep, square neckline. "And purple velvet violets at the shoulder," Miss Amanda said, sketching it all out on a pad. "Quite simple, though the skirt must be ample for dancing."

"But, Miss Amanda, I don't know how to dance." I planned to slip away at the first opportunity.

"You will manage perfectly well among the village clodhoppers," she said. Then she ordered me to bring Betty to her.

The idea of the ball awed Betty. But Miss Amanda told her, "Mind you, you must snare this Sampson man on your own. We can do no more than put a winning card or two into your hand."

Betty's dress was one of Miss Amanda's castoffs. Pink

silk, with rosettes on the skirt. Granny Thorne did the fitting for Betty's more ample figure. And suddenly the evening of the Ventnor Tradesmen's Ball arrived.

Miss Amanda helped me dress and even saw me down to the drive where Mr. Salter and his sister, Winifred, waited for me. John Thorne was to see Betty to the ball a little later. On the way I huddled on the backseat of George Salter's motorcar. The howling wind made conversation impossible, and I was thankful. All I knew of Miss Salter, a plain woman, was that she kept house for her widowed brother and looked after his son Willie in a large cottage on the grounds of the home farm. If she knew the game that Betty and I were playing at, she gave no sign. She said only, "My brother and I keep farmers' hours. Will it suit you to leave the dance early?" I told her it would suit me very well.

The ballroom was ablaze with light, and magnolia leaves and paper garlands hung from the chandeliers. As I entered with the Salters, an unknown voice from the crowd said quite clearly, "Just look, it's Miss Amanda Whitwell!"

But then Mr. Hubert Sampson, in black evening clothes and a tight collar, was there, breathless at my elbow. "Oh I say, Miss Cooke!" he gasped, bowing. Then, just as he asked me if I "cared to essay a waltz," an arresting couple stepped into the ballroom. Betty had arrived, clinging to John Thorne's arm.

It hadn't occurred to me that he would see her into the ballroom, nor that he'd be dressed for the occasion in a dark suit and a high collar. I could scarcely tear my eyes away from his blond hair and the set of his chin.

Mr. Sampson was riveted on Betty—a delicious version

of herself. A pink bandeau was wrapped around her brow in the manner of a tiara, and the gown was an almost alarming fit. "Could that be—Miss Prowse?" he breathed.

Of the four of us, only he was confused. In a kind of dance step, we were all in a knot and then paired off differently. Betty was leading Mr. Sampson onto the floor, and I was standing beside John Thorne.

When I declined to dance, he seemed relieved. Buoyed by the music, we moved out into the shadows of the terrace. We lingered there, looking out on the quicksilver sea under a harvest moon. Again, as on hunt day, we were thrown together by unlikely circumstances. I took it all as a sign from heaven.

John Thorne slipped his arm around my waist. Then I was in his arms, being kissed with all the roughness of that first dark night. But now I returned his kisses. Everything that had ever happened to me seemed to be pointing to this moment. If I thought of anything, it was of the Wisewoman's words that I would die and live again. I thought this must be the moment she'd foreseen.

Later, we walked down into the garden. He pressed me close, touching the curve of my ear with his lips, asking when we would be together.

When? Now I knew the passion that must have overcome Betty. It must only be marriage, I thought, as millions of girls had thought before me. I was willing to mingle my fate with this stranger's. Aren't two people always strangers until they are one?

"We'll be married, then," John said, reading my thoughts. The gruff sound of his voice became the throbbing of my heart.

"But will they allow it?" I whispered. "Miss Amanda—"

"Miss Amanda will allow it," John said. That she had *willed* it was beyond my imaginings.

John was looking through me with his gray eyes, and I saw in them a message I couldn't read. And so we parted at the door to the terrace with nothing more said.

I made my way across the room. A flash of pink silk proclaimed Betty's untiring presence on the dance floor with Hubert. Winifred Salter and her brother stood at the mirrored main doors, preparing to leave. As I drew near, I saw Winifred glance toward the whirling dancers and freeze. She seemed so shaken that I stepped up behind her to see what she was seeing. Then I caught a glimpse of two phantoms.

It seemed as if I'd never left the ballroom. It seemed I'd learned to dance and was dancing now with John. My heart hammered. For there I was on the dance floor in my new white gown banded in purple velvet. I was in John Thorne's arms, and he towered over me, and we were swirling like autumn leaves in the music. I thought I must be mad.

Winifred Salter turned, startled to find me behind her. She took my arm and marched me to the door, as if I were a sheltered child she wanted to shield from something obscene. I knew I had to go back to the ballroom, for it was John Thorne on the dance floor with—

Miss Salter felt me slipping from her grasp. "Don't let them make a fool of you!" she rasped at me. Then we were hurrying down the drive behind George Salter.

Betty returned from the ball at dawn, tireless and triumphant, bursting into song at odd moments all the next day. I was in the preoccupied state of a young girl who knows already what she's unwilling to admit. My mind hummed with unthinkable thoughts. I was exhausted by them when I took up Miss Amanda's breakfast tray.

In her room I found the dress hanging from her wardrobe door. A white dress banded in purple, with a skirt ample enough for dancing. A dress exactly like my own.

London. The name of that magical place rumbled like distant thunder. We'd spent the week in packing. Now the upper reaches of Whitwell Hall stood empty. I was more than vexed with Miss Amanda. I thought she'd lowered herself to play a silly trick on me. Deigning to dance in a dress like mine, on the arm of her own chauffeur, might have amused her, or anyone of her class. But my new longing for John Thorne made me feel mocked. In her presence I was as cold and starchy as I dared be. But it went unnoticed. She seemed so happy at the prospect of London that I thought she was longing to see Gregory Forrest again.

John Thorne saw us off on the ferryboat from Ryde. Traveling over this small expanse of sea was a wonder to me as I bustled about, settling Lady Eleanor and Miss Amanda in the enclosed saloon. But I felt miserable as John prepared to leave us.

He mentioned to Lady Eleanor that a small dressing case of Miss Amanda's was missing. With a nod to me, he walked back toward the gangplank, and I followed. The dressing case was where he'd left it to offer us an excuse to say our good-byes. He caught me in his arms and kissed me full on the mouth. Then he was handing me the case and striding down the gangplank. I wondered how I would endure a month without him. And what would happen when we were reunited. But I wondered for nothing, because plans I couldn't have guessed at were already at work well above my head.

The deck lurched, and Ryde fell away. Before I knew it, the ferry was nudging Portsmouth pier, and I was in that other, larger England I had never thought to see.

I smile to think of it now, but when the train drew into Waterloo Station, I thought the great glass roof of the terminal covered all of London. There were taxicabs, shops, restaurants, even a hotel in the twilight of the vast, smoky station. Then we rolled out of Waterloo in a taxi, and I scarcely dared glance out at all the traffic.

"Oh, do look, Miranda," Miss Amanda said, pointing to an omnibus. "There's one of Father's signs!" And indeed an advertisement on the omnibus read:

TAKE A CUP OF WHITWELL'S TEA:
MORNING NOON AND NIGHT.

In Mayfair we turned into quiet Charles Street and drew up at a town house, one of a long, tight row of houses running to a distant corner. The house was furnished fashionably, but there was little homelike about it, and Sir Timothy himself transferred to his club before the end of that day.

Not that we were short of gentlemen. They called every afternoon, filling the drawing room. Mr. Gregory Forrest called as often, I think, as Miss Amanda allowed. And when I answered the door, I always hoped it would be him. I was absurdly pleased that he remembered my name. Whether I was engaged to John Thorne or not, the thought of Mr. Forrest lightened my step.

My duties were less burdensome than in the country. And my room, at the back and the top of the house, was twice the size of my attic at Whitwell Hall. It was approached through a sewing room that was as good as a sitting room to me. From my window I could see a yard of cobblestones behind the house. Hays Mews it was called, enclosed by brick walls.

Miss Amanda and I were two days in getting her clothes unpacked. I was still curt to her. I couldn't rid myself of the vision of her dancing with John Thorne. To have a double—an alter ego—is a worrisome thought. But a double that is a mischievous spirit promises more trouble ahead. How strange it is to me now that I didn't blame John Thorne. But no, I laid all the blame at Miss Amanda's feet.

In the evening of our third day in London Miss Amanda sent for me and said, "Miranda, I am going to keep a journal. Not a diary of engagements. A proper journal to record my thoughts. Do you not think this an excellent way to occupy my mind?"

"I couldn't say, miss."

"I could and do." She arched her eyebrows. "Writing will clarify my thoughts, and I shall be able to examine my life."

"Yes, miss."

"So I ordered a book of blank pages from Asprey's in Bond Street. It is quite gorgeous, a work of art, with my name in silver leaf."

Miss Amanda produced the journal, buttery sky-blue

leather with silver corners. *Amanda Whitwell* was embossed on the cover. "Only think, Miranda," she went on, "what awful secrets will fill these virginal pages. Never dream of peeking at the contents yourself. Perhaps I should have it fitted with a lock. Servants do pry." With that she gave me a sly, sidelong look, and dismissed me for the night.

Tired as I was, I knew I wouldn't sleep. Restless London thundered beyond the sewing-room window. And I heard a motorcar bumping down the cobblestones of Hays Mews. It was the throbbing clatter of Sir Timothy's Lanchester.

I was at the window as the dark figure of John Thorne climbed down from the motorcar. I flew down the stairs, my heart leaping.

John was just opening the coach-house doors when I crossed the mews and stood silently behind him. He turned suddenly. "Amanda," he said quietly.

No, I thought, he didn't say that. I rushed into his arms to stop his lips with my own. "Miranda," he whispered, and his arms closed around me.

He led me up the iron stairway of the carriage house to the loft rooms above. I stood there, longing to know why John was here, and what it meant for the two of us. "John, do explain!" I said, in a tone I had adopted from someone else.

He looked at me as if a stranger had spoken. "What's to explain?" he said finally. "Lady Eleanor and the Duchess took it into their heads that they'd sooner be driven about London than hire a car. They sent me a wire, and here I am."

"The Duchess?"

"It's only my name for Miss Amanda." There was defiance in his voice. "The Duchess for all her high-and-mighty ways."

"Never let her know you call her that!" I was truly shocked.

John shook his head, looked away. "I watch my p's and q's around that young lady."

"Ah, but you've not always been so careful," I said boldly. "You were quick enough to dance with her at the Ventnor ball."

"You know about that, do you?" He ran a heavy hand through his hair. The look of a sulky boy blurred his manly face. "I wonder what busybody carried that tale. Forget it." And he took me in his arms again. "It's no matter."

"I saw you and Miss Amanda on the dance floor myself. How could you? Have you no pride?"

"Not much," John said, showing a rock-hard chin. "Besides, when you went out and she came in, I thought 'twas you had come back. She was in my arms before I knew the difference."

"You're a liar, John Thorne." I stepped back from him. "I couldn't have coaxed you onto that dance floor in a million years. It was the young mistress who called that tune."

"Have it your own way. When you know more about men than you do now, maybe you'll find out they don't take much to being accused of dancing to a woman's tune—any woman, high or low."

Especially when it's what they're doing, I thought. How could this man, so quick to hurt me, inspire such passion in me? I turned from him and walked out the door.

In her busy round of receptions and dinners, Miss Amanda seemed indifferent to my state of mind. Then she startled me by saying, "Mr. Forrest is taking me to the ballet tonight, Miranda. You have never been to the ballet of course?"

"No, miss," I said, pouring her tea. A little girl's smile played across her lips.

"You will be going as well. And don't think I have any devious plan to impersonate you. I refer to the Ventnor ball, a prank that I seem never to end paying for."

"I'm to go to the ballet as well, Miss Amanda?"

"Yes. You will sit in the gallery, so what you wear need not concern either of us. You have seen nothing of London, and this will be a little treat for you. The Russian ballet is quite new to London. Anna Pavlova is dancing *The Dying Swan* tonight."

She seemed about to dismiss me when she said, "And John Thorne will accompany you."

I went down to the kitchens lost in thought about Miss Amanda's timely plan. How could she know of the coolness that had fallen between John and me? But I was almost certain that she did. I began to suspect she heard things that only John could have told her. But I resisted knowing why it would suit her to smooth things between us. How slow I was to see her plan unfolding.

That evening I dressed Miss Amanda in her wine satin evening gown, and she had never looked more beautiful. Her black hair, drawn up into a twist, looked nearly lacquered. A touch of mascara on her eyebrow erased the small scar left from her long-ago tumble from a horse. Her mother's sable-trimmed cloak encased her in cloth of gold as thin as tissue.

After she'd gone downstairs to Mr. Forrest, I dressed hurriedly. John Thorne met me in the mews. His hands found mine and held them lightly, inviting me to draw back if I would. Then I was in his arms, and he kissed me with a gentle insistence. He gathered me nearer, gently still, certain of me once again. I pressed my face against him and savored the strength of his body, for he'd awakened something within me.

Our arms entwined, we walked to bustling Piccadilly Street and rode from there on a swaying omnibus. I was reminded of my first day in a motorcar and managed a smile.

"And what's brought the ghost of a grin out of all your solemnness, then?" John asked, quick to notice.

"I was remembering my first ride in Sir Timothy's automobile the day of the hunt. How far I thought I was from the ground."

"Ah, you were bright green with fear, and no mistake," John said, nodding wisely.

"I never showed it!"

"But you quivered from top to toe," he said. "One day I'll have you out in Sir T's auto alone. Then I'll show you what life's like at thirty miles an hour."

"Never!"

His arm slipped around my shoulders. "Or better yet, we'll have our own motor one day."

"An automobile of our own?" I said. "When I am Miss Amanda and you are the king of the Belgians!"

"Ah, not so long off as that," he said, after a quick look at me.

When the bus swerved to a stop at the Palace Theatre, we descended into a crowd of ladies encrusted with jewels and gentlemen in tall silk hats and white silk mufflers. I clung to John's hand as we climbed the stairs to the gallery, high under the dome of the theater, and fought our way toward the crowded front row.

The orchestra was suddenly gathered up by the conductor's baton into a swell of music unlike any I'd ever heard, waves of sound that made my heart soar. This was the music of the sea, with the tides ebbing and flowing, and I left Miranda Cooke behind in all the smallness of her days and ways.

The curtain rose then upon a porcelain figure, Anna Pavlova. She looked more bird than woman, more goddess than human. I sat swaying in the rhythm of her art. At the end, when the swan she had become fell dead on the stage, I wept.

I must have left the theater in a spell, for I cannot remember what more might have passed between John and me. Certainly we must have returned quickly to Charles Street, but my thoughts didn't turn on him or on Miss Amanda in that scrap of time that was mine alone.

First and last, Miss Amanda loved a sly game. I might have known she was about to reveal some news, for she summoned Miss Sybil Ward-Benedict up to town as her audience.

Miss Ward-Benedict arrived at midmorning and asked to be shown straight in to Amanda. I left them to their reunion, returning only at eleven with coffee and biscuits. Miss Amanda was saying, "I am quite done in with London and cannot face the real Season next summer."

"Then I shouldn't go through with it if I were you," Miss Ward-Benedict said gruffly. She was no lover of London. "I shan't."

"No, I suppose you won't, Sybil. But when I say that I cannot face a Season next year, I mean that I *will* not face it, and I've taken steps."

I felt Miss Amanda's eyes on me as I poured the coffee. "You see, Sybil, I have decided to become engaged to Mr. Gregory Forrest."

Miss Ward-Benedict barely covered her surprise. "So, it's to be Forrest, is it? Has he spoken to your father?"

Miss Amanda hooted. "Oh, Sybil, nobody has spoken to Father in years, on any subject! But you may be sure that Gregory has *spoken* to my mother and she has *spoken* at length in reply. I shall be more than glad to put an end to all this underground maneuvering."

"Ruddy odd reason for marrying," Miss Ward-Benedict

remarked thoughtfully. Then she said, pointedly, "When is it to be, Amanda? You won't convince me that you're serious unless you can name a date!"

Miss Amanda shifted uncomfortably in her bed. "I haven't set the date. As I'm to marry an American, I might well slip away to New York and be wed there, to deprive my mother of her hour of triumph!" Miss Amanda's eyes glittered, then darkened. "There is another wedding to be worked out before mine. Perhaps two of them."

"Whose, for heaven's sake?" Miss Ward-Benedict demanded.

"It seems that one of our downstairs maids—Betty— is pregnant and has trapped a likely man to marry her." Miss Amanda's eyes were trained on me. "And I shouldn't be surprised if Miranda didn't marry soon too. I suspect something between Miranda and our man-of-all-work down on the Isle. Thorne is his name. And to let matters drag on will simply lead to problems of Betty's sort—"

"That is *surely* her business," Miss Ward-Benedict said, embarrassed on my behalf.

"Please, miss," I heard myself say. "May I withdraw?"

Miss Amanda sighed. "Miranda, you're not to take to heart everything I say when I am attempting to amuse. I would be lost without you. I am quite serious when I say I shall want you with me always. I can see no reason why you and I should not have everything that . . . will make us both happy." And then she dismissed me.

I withdrew, raging at her calculated cruelty. When she'd said that I would remain in her service always, I'd nearly shuddered. But in her thoughtlessness, she had seemed to overlook something. If she went to New York with Mr. Forrest, surely I could not both marry John Thorne and remain with her.

I was so lost in these thoughts that I found myself standing at the head of the stairs. Nevertheless I noticed Mr. Gregory Forrest waiting below. Some secret part of me always longed for a glimpse of him.

A change came over me during our last London days. I began to think myself very worldly and I became remarkably grown-up in my manner. If I melted in John Thorne's arms, I melted a bit more slowly. And I came to what I thought were new terms with Miss Amanda. When she raged, I clucked in patient disapproval. When she played the child, I played the nanny. But she could find no fault in me because I grew more silently efficient.

As the days slipped away, Miss Amanda remained serious about announcing her engagement to Mr. Forrest. And the great day came, rather like the breaking of a long fever—a relief to all concerned.

An engagement party was planned for one of our last London evenings. That morning a parcel from Asprey's came for Miss Amanda. It was a large traveling jewel case lavishly bound in gold. On the lid were stamped a small A and a W, and a central initial more boldly emblazoned: F for Forrest. Inside were a dozen drawers and trays lined in pale suede.

When I went up to see to Miss Amanda's hair for that evening, I barely knocked before entering her room. And there I saw Mr. Forrest. He stood behind Miss Amanda, fastening a necklace of pearls around her neck, the second of his engagement gifts in a single day.

Mr. Forrest met my eye. He favored me with a crooked smile and then, of all things, gave me a wink. I smiled in return before composing myself.

"Gregory!" Miss Amanda was saying, "what will my maid think to find you here? You've no idea how high-minded she is."

"How can she be less than an angel when she looks so much like you?" he asked, and to me, "I hope you wish us well, Miranda."

I was too dazzled by him to reply. Miss Amanda turned, and her eyebrows rose high at my silence. She was standing before Mr. Forrest and drew his arms possessively around herself.

"Oh, sir," I managed, "I wish you every happiness."

"And maybe you'll do me a favor, Miranda," Mr. Forrest said in a voice of genial gruffness.

"Anything, sir," I murmured, making Miss Amanda smile at how easily I was overcome by him.

"Maybe you can convince Amanda of the wisdom of a short engagement. Persuade her there's no reason for waiting?"

"Ah, but there *are* reasons, Gregory!" Miss Amanda cut in.

But Mr. Forrest's eyes were still upon me, and I met them briefly. From a pocket he drew out a small box bound with a silk cord and held it out to me. "Here, Miranda, a small token of our engagement. It's a happy time, and you should share it."

My eyes filled at the goodness of this man, and I envied Miss Amanda. With a faltering hand I opened the box. Inside lay a slender gold chain.

It was more beautiful to me than the rope of pearls at Miss Amanda's throat. She was much amused as I tried to stammer my thanks.

"Have you something to wear on it?" Mr. Forrest asked.

"Oh, sir, I'll have my foreign coin put on it. It's the only other gift I was ever given."

"And what kind of coin is it?"

I was never without it. From my apron pocket, I drew it out.

"It's a funny thing to come across this far from home," Mr. Forrest said when I handed it to him. "An American Indianhead penny. Where did you come by it, Miranda?"

"The Wisewoman gave it to me," I said without thinking.

"Wisewoman?"

"A fortune-teller," Miss Amanda said. "You have no idea how superstitious simple people are in this country, Gregory."

"I doubt Miranda consulted the fortune-teller. It's surely customary for the client to do the paying."

"She was a lonely old woman who was being kind," I murmured, and a bond strengthened between me and Mr. Forrest.

"Was she kind enough to foresee your future?" he asked.

"She spoke strangely," I said. "I doubt I remember much."

"I'll bet you remember some," Mr. Forrest said, drawing me out. "People do, even when they aren't believers."

"I remember one thing very clearly, sir. The Wise-woman said I would marry twice."

"Marry *twice*, Miranda?" Miss Amanda laughed mockingly. "My dear, I shall do very well to get you married *once!*"

Early in December of 1911 we returned to the island I had never thought to leave. But the events begun in London swept away all thoughts of a quiet winter there. Miss Amanda wore an enormous square-cut diamond ring, and she and Lady Eleanor began to plan an engagement party. We'd left Mr. Forrest behind in London, and my mind was free of frivolous thoughts of him, though under my collar I wore the new chain with the old coin fixed on it.

The servants' hall gave me a watchful welcome. Betty was nowhere about, and I hadn't the courage to ask after her. I feared the worst.

From the first hour my young mistress kept me so busy that Mrs. Creeth herself forced a fortifying cup of tea on me late that night. "That young miss'll work you to death," she said in all kindness. "Here, drink this."

When Mrs. Creeth went off to her bed, I settled by the kitchen hearth with the cup in my hand. And I thought of John Thorne. What would I have done if I'd known that at that very moment he was standing in Miss Amanda's room while she held out to him the hand that bore Mr. Forrest's engagement ring?

Then I heard a sound from the door, and Willie Salter slipped in from the cold. "Whatever brings you here at this hour, Willie?" I asked, startled.

"A word from Betty," he said. "She'd have written except she don't know how. She's living with us now and says to come to the home farm on your first half day."

I remembered Winifred Salter from the night of the Ventnor ball and was astonished that she'd taken Betty in. I promised Willie that I'd come to see Betty at my first opportunity, and he vanished into the night.

Whitwell Hall was drawing in these days against the gray winter. As Miss Amanda's engagement party drew nearer, she kept me too busy to think, even of John Thorne, and I scarcely saw him. But I managed half an afternoon to visit the home farm.

Winifred Salter herself opened the door to greet me and offered me tea later before she disappeared. When Betty entered the Salters' sitting room, no dressmaking could now disguise her condition. "Ooo!" she cried. "You been gone a donkey's years!"

And there on Betty's hand was a narrow gold wedding band. She grinned impishly. "That's right. I'm Mrs. Hubert Sampson!"

"But if you are, why are you here?"

"Oh, orl right, if you must know everythin' at once," she said. "It orl started wiv me tryin' to dazzle Hubert at the Ventnor ball. Miss Salter didn't approve of that, but she took an interest in my situation. Once you were orf to London, she turned up at the Hall for a private word with Mr. Finley himself. Then he told me to pack up and follow Miss Salter home and do as she said."

Betty's eyes grew round. "Well, Miss Salter sent her brother to fetch Hubert. She went straight to the point with him, saying I'd make a good wife, and dutiful too! She told him he'd been a loving son to his mother, but if he didn't take steps soon, he'd have no one when his mother was dead.

"Then she made it clear I was in a particular situation. She said that Hubert could make up for lost time by marrying a ready-made family, in a manner of speaking. I thought this would run him orf for sure. But Miss Salter asked him if he thought he could do better. That clinched things. We was married in the registry office at Shanklin.

"It's orl very hush-hush, you see. Miss Salter wouldn't hear of me coming up against Hubert's old ma now. When the baby's born, then we'll tell her we're married."

"But won't she be angry that you've been going behind her back?" I asked.

"Very likely, but what can she do? She'll have to knuckle under if she expects Hubert to provide a roof over her head."

"And Hubert. Doesn't he mind at all about the baby?"

"Mind? Why, he talks about it like it was his own." Betty beamed. And I didn't know whether to laugh or cry.

During the week of the engagement party, I found a reason to visit Smuggler's Cottage. The Hall was filling with houseguests, and Mr. Finley was snappish. My excuse for a stolen hour with Granny Thorne was a new tablecloth that needed hemming.

Her welcome was as warm as her hearth, and she was a keen audience for my news from the Hall. At midnight, following the family celebrations of the engagement, there was to be a bonfire on the hill, and fireworks.

She listened with all her ears, but said, "I'll keep to the hearth that night, but I'll raise a glass of my own wine to Miss Amanda and her young man."

Her eyes had flickered to a spot above my head. I didn't know that John Thorne had come home for his tea and was standing silently behind me. "Yes," Granny said. "I am better off in my own cottage. I need but one thing to put my mind at rest."

Granny's old eyes glowed brightly. "Miranda, all I need to die happy is to see you in this cottage as one of my own family." Then John announced himself with a scrape of his boot, and I knew he had heard her words.

Granny and I prepared a tea for ourselves and John in the little kitchen. As I was slicing a loaf, her voice piped, "It's said there's never room for two women at one hearth-side. But that's a load of old rubbish. There'll be room for you here, and more room later, as I won't live forever."

"Gran, you're saying too much," John's voice boomed from the other room, and both Granny and I jumped.

When we carried in the tray, I found myself at a family tea, as if all were decided. And when the afternoon ended, John walked me back to the Hall through the lowering twilight.

Deep in the grove, he muttered, "Gran's old. But still strong. She may live a long time yet. We'll not be spending the whole of our married life under her roof."

Something stirred within me. I was ready for love, and John spoke as if it were all decided between us. The evening wind seemed to blow less cold. "We'll start out with her," he said, "but there's other opportunities elsewhere."

"But where shall we go?"

"The century's young, like us, and it's a big world." Words forsook him, but somehow I saw what he wanted me to see. A world of steam and speed and chances, even for us. It was a dream of underlings. I thought I saw freedom for us.

"There's America," he said, but that was too distant to draw me. Now in the kitchen yard, light from Miss Amanda's window fell upon us, and he was fumbling in a pocket. He withdrew a gold ring, worn to a thread, with a single stone, a ruby like a drop of blood. "It was Gran's and then my mother's. Now it's yours."

The ring fit my finger perfectly. It gave me the courage to ask. "But when—"

"Soon now. There's no reason to wait longer."

How little I remember of the night of the engagement party. My mind was on my own concerns. If Miss Amanda, radiant in her silver gown, noticed my ring, she made no sign. Of course she saw! If my engagement hadn't been her own plan, she'd have put a stop to it.

I worked through the evening under Mr. Finley's snapping fingers until midnight. Then the villagers set alight the bonfire, and the guests assembled on the Hall steps. Champagne was handed around. The staff were free for a few moments to watch the bonfire and the first fireworks.

From somewhere John stepped up beside me, taking my hand with his ring upon it. We stood there, undeniably together now. Then after distant thunder, the night sky blossomed with white fire.

I married John Thorne in the first week of the new year, 1912.

Miss Amanda made no reference to my plans, but in the last days before the wedding she had given me my afternoons off, to make my meager preparations. I was to wear a practical costume cast off by Miss Amanda, a dark jacket and skirt. They fit me like a glove.

On the day John and I were to be married, Miss Amanda broke her silence. Even after all these years, I'm angry with myself for remembering her words more clearly than the clergyman's. But perhaps that's fitting, for what was in her mind cast a longer shadow than my wedding vows that bound me to John Thorne for so brief a time.

I had taken in her breakfast tray to find her looking ill. Her hair was damp against the pillow, and a faint sour smell hung in the room. "Shall I call Dr. Post, Miss Amanda?" I asked.

"I am no more ill than I should be, nor is this the first morning." Then she said even more abruptly, "You are to marry Thorne today. I wish you well, Miranda. It could not suit me better. I should have been glad to see you marry sooner, but there were reasons why—it is never wise to rush into anything so terribly permanent."

"If you say so, miss," I replied. Then she fell silent. I left her presence, and she did not see me again until I was a married woman. But in this I had not drawn farther from her, but nearer.

AMANDA SPEAKS

I am Amanda Whitwell, and I have been intimidated by very little in my nineteen years. I shan't begin by being cowed by a blank page. I shall write in this diary as I speak. I do not write for the eye of anyone now living. But in time, when all the chains that bind young women have fallen away, my book will find its proper reader. I shall head this, my first entry:

THE NEW YEAR, 1912

For it is in this newly born year that I mean to complete the plan for my life.

Miranda, as I call her—you see I named her myself—had dropped out of nowhere, really, and it was like a joke played by fate. She looked enough like me to be my twin. In all her boundless innocence, she had clearly been sent to solve my quite complicated problems. Problems caused by another ser-

vant, who had given me the only real joy I had ever known. I can't think when I first fell in love with him. John Thorne is his name, and very handsome in his brutal way. I must have been a child, for John is ten years and more my senior.

We Whitwells belong to a dying class, as I notice from my mother's meaningless gentility. There cannot be another generation like my mother's. Not in this family. For I have no intention of dancing to Lady Eleanor's stately minuet. I hear a wilder music in my mind.

Sometimes I suspect my mother thinks me mad. How little she knows me! Certainly she is anxious to tame me into marriage. And if I am a bit ill in the mornings, she either does not notice, or dares not.

My plan has a lovely shape, and nothing can stop it now. I have sent my fiancé, Gregory Forrest, back to America to await my arrival. I won't remain suffocated in England, where I could never be sure of holding John Thorne forever. Sooner or later we would be discovered and pilloried upon the class system. But in wild, far-flung America, where a servant's role is scarcely understood and I shall be a foreigner, John Thorne will be mine on my terms. And I shall have Gregory as well, to provide for me. For it is my plan that John, with his respectable wife, will join me and my husband as our chauffeur and maid.

How lovely it will be—the long drives through endless, golden afternoons. Once we are in a secluded spot, I shall rap on the window that divides us, and we shall enjoy an interlude in some hidden park. All the rest of my life will be a golden afternoon, while my husband will go about his tiresome business and John's wife will attend to my more trivial needs.

It is quite dark now, and the hours drag on terribly. Where are they now, my lover and my maid, who have been married today? Will they spend their wedding night in some crossroads inn or return to the cottage?

I won't torture myself with these thoughts. After all, it's my plan, and Miranda lacks the spark to ignite the fires within John Thorne. Only I can do that. And I'm not really alone. I am carrying John Thorne's child, and he knows. I wanted his child to bind us together, to bring him to his knees finally.

The middle of April seems just the time for my marriage to Gregory. All will look well at first. And later—poor Gregory will be called a rake by his New York friends when they learn how scandalously soon his little English bride presents him with an heir. But Gregory is the least of my concerns. It's the price he must pay for the wife he desires so much more than she desires him. Without this child, John and I might drift apart. And that must never be.

JANUARY 15, 1912

The sickness of the mornings has passed, and I'm feeling fit and still willow-slim. I do a little dance of triumph around my room even on these cold mornings. But Miranda is at the door now, and I must compose myself. Her dignity mounts daily, and her voice grows steadily more like an echo of my own.

There are letters from New York on my breakfast tray, and I wonder that Gregory Forrest can build his houses and still write so much. My delay makes him restless. He includes two steamship tickets—for Miss Whitwell and her maid for an April tenth sailing from Southampton. And if that were not

*enough, a brochure from the White Star Line about its new
liner.*

Yes, I shall sail on the maiden voyage of that ship.

*A sign from heaven that my plan is meant to be! Dear,
bumbling Father has revealed his generous wedding gift—a
Rolls-Royce automobile! A limousine, and that of course re-
quires a British chauffeur. Poor Father hadn't realized that I
could hardly take Miranda to America as my maid without
Thorne. Once reminded of this, he offered me the pair of them,
rather like a pair of Ming vases that it would be a great pity to
split up!*

*Father was closeted in his study with Miranda and
Thorne and Finley for a long time. Such a bother, when the
whole thing was really decided by me ages ago. Their meeting
went on so long that I began to suspect Miranda of making dif-
ficulties. When she came into my room later, her face was indeed wet with tears.*

*"Whatever is the matter?" I asked her, and it all came out.
It was nothing to do with New York at all. Poor, drab Betty,
who had married her draper in haste, had gone through a
normal pregnancy only to lose the child. And soon after, she'd
died herself.*

*What a relief that Miranda was not disturbed at the
thought of going to New York. That* would *have been awkward.*

*Last night John Thorne came to my room. It seems that
nothing can hurry the Rolls-Royce people, and the limousine
will not be ready to ship until early summer. So Thorne must*

stay behind and accompany the auto on a ship to New York when it's ready.

How angry this makes me! But John convinced me that it will look much better all around if Miranda and I arrive in New York alone.

APRIL 7, 1912

I might have known! Everything was going too well. And now a last-minute complication just as I was counting the hours.

John Thorne and I have been discovered.

It is all because I was overtired and growing careless. Though of course it was not really my fault. It only happened because Mother and Father would give a tiresome bon voyage party for me on my last Saturday.

After the party John came to my room. It was nearly the last moment we could be together. Surely I deserved something after enduring that wretched party. Later I fell asleep without sending him away. I awoke at eight o'clock, and there was John, still heavily asleep beside me. I shook him, and he awoke suddenly. How was I to get him out of a house already astir? And in that moment Miranda opened the door to bring my early-morning tea.

All my plans seemed threatened. It was all too, too unfair. Thorne drew away from me as if I were some loathsome beast. He threw his legs over the side of the bed and sat there, turned away from us both, his head in his hands.

Miranda stood in the doorway, rigid as a statue, looking in on this absurd scene. No one spoke. John was incapable of doing anything. He sat there, his great naked back casting a long shadow across my bed.

Perhaps it is as well she knows. She was bound to know

one day, however blind she chose to be. But I shall never let myself be caught again, never.

I heard my voice saying, "I should think, all things considered, that we shall need another cup for morning tea. Go and fetch it at once, Miranda."

I even managed to meet her gaze. Her eyes had gone quite dark. From violet to near black. She looked quite changed. Quite thoroughly changed.

Early on Wednesday, April 10, 1912, I, Miranda Cooke Thorne, stood again on the platform of Waterloo Station in London. But I was not the same young girl who had gaped at that scene the previous autumn. For I'd lost everything in my world. My husband was neither his own man nor mine, and our marriage was a mockery. He had stirred the beginnings of my passion but had touched me nowhere else. When I found him in another woman's bed, I was through with lying to myself. The last of my innocence was driven out, and I expect it showed.

I'd said nothing to John Thorne that morning. I stared at his naked back while she struggled to cover herself. I spoke not a word to him in the half week before I left for London. At Smuggler's Cottage I packed my few belongings into a satchel while John Thorne wavered in the doorway, searching, perhaps, for words that would have changed nothing. I walked out past him without a backward look.

I said little more to the servants at Whitwell Hall, for I couldn't be sure what *they* knew. On the day I left, I'd have walked straight past even Mrs. Creeth if she hadn't reached out quickly to embrace me. "It's hard to be going off to strange parts," she said. "And harder still to leave behind your friend in a fresh grave. I know you was a true friend to Betty."

My eyes swam with tears. "I shall remember Betty as a friend in a friendless world," I half whispered. "And I shall remember your kindness in this last moment. There's nothing more I'll want to remember."

At Waterloo I waited on the platform. The hand luggage had already been put on the boat train. I carried only Miss Amanda's jewel case—a gift from Mr. Forrest— and a bag that contained the leather book she wrote in occasionally. I longed to be off, even though I must go with the person I hated most in the world. I never thought of escape from her. I had nowhere to go. And I was a married woman in the eyes of the law. That was another chain that bound me.

Miss Amanda stood apart from me with her mother and some London friends. There'd been another farewell party, at Charles Street, and faithful Miss Ward-Benedict had stayed on to see us away. Miss Amanda was dressed in a spring coat and short whipcord skirt. Her coat was loosely belted, for she was not the willow wand she'd been. From the time I'd found her ill, so much like Betty, I knew she was carrying a child, and now I knew who the father was.

Because these last moments hung heavy on me, I drew

from my coat pocket the leaflet that advertised the famous ship we were to sail in. I began to read, "The *Titanic* will depart on her maiden voyage from Southampton. . . ."

As the White Star Line boat train rolled out of Waterloo, I sat with my back to the engine, facing Miss Amanda, the jewel case firmly on my knees for safekeeping. How she must have dreaded a journey with me! But in our compartment we were surrounded by Americans, and she allowed herself to be caught up in conversation with the lady beside her. I was interested in her too and would have been far more interested had I known my fate and the fate of this stranger were to be entwined—long after I was free of Miss Amanda.

She was Miss Rebecca Reed of New York, a journalist who supported herself by her pen and her curiosity. Not yet thirty, she was at home in the world and spoke with the experience of twice her years.

Miss Reed was not handsome, but she wore glossy furs and a hat with an enormous black and white striped bow that escaped the outrageous by a hairbreadth. "What fun," she was saying, "to cross on the *Titanic*. I'd have booked first-class passage with my last dollar for the joy of rubbing elbows with all those Social Register types!"

Miss Amanda blanched at the mention of money and the thought of rubbed elbows. But the blanching British didn't bother Miss Reed. "Even if you're not traveling with any of your menfolk, you'll find plenty of courtly swains to look out for you on the crossing. It's a perfectly respectable custom, you know."

She took a moment to withdraw from her hand luggage a peculiar, not very handsome stuffed toy to show

Miss Amanda. A music box in the shape of a pig and too realistic to be droll. She twisted the tail, and the pig played a tinkling tune. "One of the glories of the *Titanic*," she said, "is that it's unsinkable. Still, I go nowhere without my lucky pig!"

Then she whispered that the young couple sitting among us, a Mr. and Mrs. Daniel Marvin, were returning from their wedding trip. The wedding ceremony, it seems, had been cinematographed as a moving picture. Mr. Marvin's father was the head of an important American cinematograph company.

Miss Reed went on to describe other notable passengers on the ship. The Wideners and the Fortunes and the Ryersons and the Strauses, Major Archibald Butt and the Thayers and the Countess of Rothes. And against this roll call of the mighty, I passed the remainder of our train journey.

I rejoiced bitterly at the miles separating me from John Thorne. I vowed if he followed me—followed *her*—into our new life, I would never let him touch me again. I would be no one's easy convenience. I would play my role as lady's maid and no more, until the moment when I would rise up. I only hoped I'd know that moment when it came. And I rather thought I would.

The passengers began to stir. The train shuddered to a stop at Southampton. We were beside the quay. Above us, seventy feet out of the water, loomed what seemed the largest creation ever wrought by man: the *Titanic*.

When we left the moorings, the ship seemed not to move at all. It only throbbed gently like a great, gilded whale breathing deep in its throat.

I lost myself in the duties I was to perform. Servants seemed to outnumber passengers in this astonishing floating city of endless corridors and grand stairways that rang with the easy laughter of the very rich. I stood in the line of ladies' maids at the purser's counter, where a ransom in jewels was to be banked in the ship's safe by a Mr. McElroy.

I spent the rest of the afternoon settling my young lady in her stateroom on B deck. It was compact, but luxurious, with a four-poster bed, a dressing table, and even hot water piped directly in. My cabin, between Miss Amanda's and the main corridor, was scarcely less comfortable.

At the forward end of our corridor was the grand staircase, the central crossroads of the ship. Above it was a great clock set in under a glass dome from which daylight struck at the heart of the ship. At the other end of the corridor was a French restaurant, an alternative to the main dining saloon on D deck below. It was filled with French furniture of a bygone century, grouped in an ocean of white linen. Beyond the silk-draped bays on one side was the less formal Café Parisien, with wicker furniture and potted palms. And beyond or beneath it all were a Turkish bath and ballrooms and lounges and smoking rooms and writing rooms—more luxury than I had ever imagined.

I dressed my young lady for tea in a gown with a large bouquet of silk flowers at the waist, then attended to her hair. Our eyes never met in the looking glass. My hands stung from having to touch her. When she was ready to join her fellow passengers, she wrenched her diamond engagement ring from her finger. "Put it in the safe with the rest of my jewelry. I do not choose to be an engaged woman during the crossing." Then she was gone, and the lovely, meaningless diamond lay winking in my palm.

After a trip to the safe, I went to the open promenade of A deck above, to stand in the sea winds and watch the coastline slide past. I caught a scent of land, of England in April, and I seemed to know where we were.

Yes, this was the Isle of Wight sweeping by. And there was Shanklin pier, not five miles from where I was born. And Dunnose Hill, where my father's wagon had lost its wheel. I couldn't see the Wisewoman's cottage, but I could hear again her prophecy. *"Your future lies . . . beyond a mountain of ice, where you will die and live again. I see you in a world so strange and distant . . ."*

The ship knifed on with uncanny speed. There ahead was one last pier. Ventnor, where Betty and I had had our photograph made.

But I would look no more. I knew I would never go back. Already I was drawing the glove off my left hand. I twisted the worn ruby ring off my finger. Never mind that it had once been Granny Thorne's. John Thorne had put it on my hand, and it had no business being there. He had never given me a wedding band. Perhaps Miss Amanda had forgotten to tell him to give me one. I dropped the ruby ring over the side, into the churning sea.

The *Titanic* was like a small world in the great universe of the Atlantic. A journey on it was a little lifetime. A bugle sounded to announce every meal, and the ladies changed their clothes as often as if they were visiting a country house. The orchestra played graceful melodies, and after each meal the lounges were thronged with friends gathered to drink their coffee. In this false, beautiful shipboard world, even I was treated with great civility.

In a sort of drawing room set aside for servants, I was soon on pleasant terms with Miss Annie Robinson, the stewardess in our corridor, and with Mademoiselle Victorine, the French maid of Mrs. Ryerson, wife of the American steel magnate. Annie told me harmless gossip about the passengers, including the tall, languid Colonel John Jacob Astor, who was honeymooning with a bride younger than his own son, Vincent. Like the Ryersons, the Astors had boarded the ship in Cherbourg, and so had their friend Mrs. Margaret Brown, a wealthy American. Victorine was a fashion plate and the soul of propriety.

Miss Amanda's beauty did not go unnoticed. Miss Reed had been right about a lady traveling alone. Miss Amanda was surrounded by swains of all sorts, eager to shelter her from the hardships of this luxurious voyage, and she was determined to be a carefree young girl again.

Her admirers included Mr. Jack Thayer of Philadelphia, a handsome boy of no more than seventeen, and Major Archibald Butt, the American president Taft's military aide. But my young lady had settled on a different kind of "protector," who was neither as courtly nor as respectable as the others. He was Mr. Clem Sawyer of San Francisco, and he was by far the handsomest man on the *Titanic*.

On Friday they dined in the Café Parisien, and I waited up for her till two o'clock in the morning. On Saturday night it was later still. I opened a porthole for the brisk ocean air to keep me awake. The weather was growing colder every minute.

There was a knock and Miss Reed stood at the door, looking agitated. I asked her to step inside, though my young lady had not returned.

"How well I know!" Miss Reed threw herself into a chair. "Your name is Miranda, isn't it?"

"Yes, miss."

"Are you a married lady?"

I hesitated, and she noticed. "Yes, miss."

"Well, I suppose that should put me at my ease a little," she replied. "I know I'm a busybody, but the fact is, Miranda, that your Amanda Whitwell is about to disgrace herself. The kind of people on this ship pretend to be tolerant, but they are as stiff-necked as a Quaker meeting, with the forgiving spirit left out. Many of them will see Amanda again in New York. But they'll refuse to know her if she makes a fool of herself with Clem Sawyer. Good grief! Sawyer's a famous menace with women. His usual taste runs more to chorus girls and worse. But a young lady. . . ." Miss Reed seemed nearly overcome with concern.

"I suppose your Amanda has led a sheltered life up to now, and is carried away with that good-looking devil. But, Miranda," she continued in a rush, "can't you have a word with her? Just to warn her. I know how close Englishwomen are to their maids. You even look alike! The poor child doesn't know the danger she's in."

I smiled bitterly to myself. Should I tell Miss Reed that no man on earth could have the least influence over Amanda Whitwell? That she was maddened by self-love and ruined already? No. I couldn't tell the truth. Miss Reed would have thought me crazed. I stood there, silent, like any tongue-tied servant, and Miss Reed only sighed.

At that moment Miss Amanda entered the room. Her

face was blurred with champagne and she staggered slightly. But then she turned a bright, mechanical smile on Miss Reed, who soon beat a hasty retreat.

"What did she want?" my young lady demanded as the door was closing behind Miss Reed.

"I couldn't say, miss."

"Oh, couldn't you? You have very little to say for yourself these days. However convenient you are to me, Miranda, I advise you not to take advantage of my good disposition. You're becoming a bore, and a terrible prig into the bargain."

"I expect you are tired, miss," I said in an empty voice.

"I am very tired indeed, mostly of you." She tore at the pearls looped around her neck till they jerked loose. She threw them at a chair. Her eyes never left me, and I saw so much madness in them that I could scarcely hold my ground.

"Shall I speak to the stewardess about drawing your bath, miss?"

"You shall speak to *me*," she barked, "and truthfully, about what that Rebecca Reed was doing here." She dropped her voice, for she must have heard it echoing about the stateroom like a fishwife's. "Do not make me ask you again."

After a lengthy pause I said, "She came in friendship, miss. She fears your association with a certain gentleman on the ship has left you open to criticism."

"The certain gentleman being Mr. Sawyer, I trust."

"Yes, miss, so I believe."

She hooted with false laughter. "That pathetic old

maid! What wouldn't Rebecca Reed do for one idle glance from a man like Clem Sawyer? What did you tell her when she was kind enough to meddle in my affairs?"

"It was not my place to tell her anything, miss."

"How right you are to remember that, Miranda. Yet, what *would* you have told her if you had not been such a mealymouthed, sniveling little servant?"

"I would have told her, miss, that if anyone needed protection, it would be Mr. Sawyer."

Her eyes went black. She stepped toward me, and all I could see was her distorted face. Her hand flashed, and she struck me with all her might. "You insolent, pious little upstart," she whispered. But her words came from a great distance. The great gap that had always been there between us opened up at last to reveal its depths. I was still the servant. But Amanda Whitwell had finally lost control of herself—giving me a terrible glimpse of my future in her grip. Now she'd come past being able to manipulate others without showing her hand. "Not another word from you," she said in a low, hateful voice. "I will not hear your voice until we are docked in New York and must make a favorable impression upon Mr. Forrest. And no, you are not to ring the stewardess for my bath. I shall not be sleeping in my stateroom tonight."

She turned to jerk open the cabin door. Clem Sawyer stood there, a study in black and white. He was a tall, lithe figure in evening clothes. A spiral of smoke rose from his cigarette. He reached out to claim her, slipping his arm around her thickened waist. The door closed behind them.

Sunday, April 14, 1912, was a brisk, brilliant day upon the gray, shadowless sea. I entered my young lady's stateroom at the regular hour, mainly out of habit. It was empty, of course.

I picked up the pearls from the chair and returned them to the suede bag where they were kept. I laid out my young lady's clothes for the day and went to leave the necklace with the purser.

I felt footloose with an odd freedom that Sunday morning. As I was taking a turn on the boat deck, bundled in a thick scarf, I met the Countess of Rothes's maid. We stood chatting for a while in the shelter of the davits that held the lifeboats in place. At midday I returned to my young lady's stateroom to find that she'd been there, changed her clothes, and gone away again. I wondered if she was making herself scarce because of me. She'd decreed that I not speak to her. Perhaps it had occurred to her that there would be unnatural silences now.

But that evening she was waiting for me to dress her for dinner. "I shall not wear the black tonight." She paused, waiting. "Black is all the rage among the American women." Another pause as I stood silent. "The pink, I think," she said at last.

I drew out the long pink gown, and she reached for it. She was, I suppose, determined to show that she could give herself careful attention, and she managed to get into the gown on her own. She even found a pair of silver slippers and plunged her feet into them. "I won't require jewelry," she said to her looking glass. And she took her long fur wrap and made good her escape, though the bugle from the dining room would not sound for quite another half hour.

We were trapped, she and I, in the middle of the ocean, on a vast ship that had become too small. I wondered how we would last out this voyage in quarters growing ever closer. For we'd gone beyond the point of no return with each other.

But I was never to be in that stateroom with her again.

That night there was hymn singing in the second-class dining saloon. Victorine was there, and she and I shared a hymnal. Afterward we strolled the boat deck. Victorine was discretion itself in her talk of the Ryersons and their three children. I was discreet to the point of stony silence about Miss Whitwell, and I expect Victorine noticed.

"I wonder where Mademoiselle Reed is keeping herself this evening?" she was saying now. "Inside, out of the cold, perhaps. And she travels with that small musical pig! Is it not amusing?" She laughed.

But I couldn't pay attention to her. The sea's immense emptiness drew all my thoughts. The Atlantic that night was as calm as the mere at Whitwell Hall. Somehow it called to me, but I turned from its silent voice. Our teeth chattered with the cold.

Farther along the deck a couple stood together beside the rail. I saw the long fur wrap and silver slippers, and I walked quickly past the pair. But Victorine's eyebrows were high. "Was that not your Mademoiselle Whitwell?"

I nodded, and she said, "Ah, she is a one, with that Mr. Clem Sawyer."

Miss Amanda had snared Mr. Sawyer for yet another night. She would betray Mr. Forrest again, and I would be her unwilling accomplice. But I could not think of it anymore. There was something in me that would no longer serve. There was a stranger in me struggling to be born. A self that lurked in mystery behind the matching masks she and I wore.

The night was arctic cold. Just before Victorine and I went inside, I looked up. Above us in the crow's nest a sailor stood watch. His lofty perch seemed terribly cold, very lonely, very reassuring. "Eight hundred miles to New York," I heard a strolling passenger say to his companions.

It was sometime past eleven o'clock when I returned to my cabin. Miss Amanda's stateroom was silent. There was nothing to hear except the faint whir of the ship's engines below. I drew on a flannel nightgown, a castoff of Miss Amanda's, for the rosebud pattern had faded.

I went into her room and automatically looked about for some task. I busied myself in freshening Miss Amanda's gowns, trying to remove the odor of Mr. Sawyer's cigarette smoke. But after I closed a steamer trunk that was gaping open, there was nothing more to do.

I stood there in her room as if I were waiting for something to happen. And almost at once something did. I heard a noise, and whatever it was came from far off. The room seemed to shift, and I staggered. Suddenly the ship was still, utterly still.

The hum of the engines below had stopped. I opened the door to the sound of hurrying feet in the passageway. I heard a steward say, "Ice." Then the engines ground into life again, a curious half life, and labored. I sat down in a chair, neither alarmed nor quite comfortable.

But in the next moment Victorine was at the door. "Oh, Miranda," she said wildly, "my lady—Madame Ryerson—is in such a state! I must go back at once, but I come to tell you. The steward, he was at Monsieur and Madame Ryerson's door. He says there is a great iceberg, and we have stopped so we do not run it down!"

"Is it serious?" I asked her.

"Oh, no. This ship cannot sink. But everyone is pouring onto the decks. It is said there is ice everywhere!"

Then she was gone. I stood there, undecided, and staggered again as the stateroom tipped slightly toward the port side. A glass fell from a shelf and shattered. I returned to my room and drew on my stockings and shoes. I was about to reach for my dress when the stewardess burst in. "You are to put on your life preserver at once. Captain Smith's orders." She took a cork vest from the cabinet and fitted it onto me, jerking the straps tight at the waist. "Where is Miss Whitwell?"

"I couldn't say," I answered.

"When she returns, put her life preserver on her as I have done yours." Then she stopped in the doorway and looked back. "Put on a warm coat over the preserver. And you might go to Mr. McElroy and get Miss Whitwell's jewelry, if it is in his care."

My fitted gray wool coat would not go over the cork vest. I went without it, my faded nightgown billowing beneath the vest, into the crowded corridor. Most people either wore their life preservers or were struggling with them. Several who had perhaps drunk too much were laughing. Others had not been persuaded to don anything that would spoil the lines of their dinner clothes.

There was a mob scene on C deck around the purser's counter when I got there. Mr. McElroy was handing over the jewelry as quickly as possible. He gave me Miss Amanda's in an untidy mound, and I bore it away, terrified that I would drop something.

I managed to make my way back up to B deck against the tide of people surging along the corridor. At my cabin door, I saw the Ryerson family. Mr. Ryerson was leading his wife, a son of perhaps twelve or thirteen, their two daughters, their governess, and Victorine. She alone was without a life preserver.

She dropped behind and clutched my arm. "Your young lady, do you know where she is?"

I shook my head.

"Then let us hope she finds herself protected by a gentleman who knows the meaning of chivalry."

"Are we in real danger?" I whispered.

"We are told to be tranquil, and yet it is said the mailbags are floating in the hold. The stokers have forsaken the furnaces and are swarming upward," she replied. "We are in the hands of God." Then she hurried away.

Miss Amanda's stateroom was as I had left it. She had not come for her life preserver, and I knew in my heart where she was. She would have made it her business to be in Mr. Sawyer's bed by now. I lingered, thinking the room made a safer refuge than the teeming corridors. The lamps still blazed, yet the whole unsinkable ship was standing at a frightening angle. Perhaps I still waited there, the jewelry in my hands, because these were the last moments of my servitude.

The stewardess appeared again in the doorway. "What? Not gone already? Everybody up on deck. Ladies in the lifeboats on the port side!"

Panic was growing in me. I let the jewelry fall in a scatter across the dressing table. Then, without thought of a warm wrap, I bolted out the door.

A band of steerage passengers, their faces strained, were being led along by a crew member. I noticed that the men's boots were gushing water and the women's skirts were wet to the knees.

We were led up to A deck, where I found a group of first-class passengers and servants, including the Ryersons and Victorine. We waited for a lifeboat to be lowered. But the windows were closed, and after a considerable time we were led up another flight to the boat deck. The higher we climbed, the more deafening was the noise. The shriek of escaping steam. The ship itself was screaming.

On the open deck the air was freezing. My eyes teared, but I struggled to make sense of the scene. Forward were the davits for four lifeboats. One, perhaps two, of the boats were gone. The figures crowding around those that remained were families, but they were parting, or being parted. Mrs. Ryerson's hands reached out in an effort to gather in all her children. Mr. Ryerson had removed his life preserver and was urging it on the protesting Victorine. No, no, she was mouthing, but he wrapped it hastily around her.

We waited again, listening to the men in our group murmuring among themselves. I eyed the lifeboats, those wooden hulls that would be like walnut shells on the ocean so far below. I saw the young Mrs. Marvin, who had traveled down in the boat train in our compartment, clinging to her new husband. His lips moved, reassuring her perhaps. He pointed down the ship to another group of lifeboats. At last she allowed him to propel her toward the boats.

Now came word that the windows on the A deck had been opened, and once again we descended the stairway. At last, using deck chairs as steps, the passengers were urged to board the lifeboat through the open windows. Mrs. Ryerson's two daughters were already in the boat.

A crewman was urging her to follow, but she held her young son's shoulders. Clearly, she would not leave him behind. She clasped him to her and turned her face away from the open boat where her other children waited. Mr. Ryerson spoke to a ship's officer, pleading with him. At last the boy was allowed to go with his mother. But after that the officer boomed, "No more boys!"

Behind me I heard Miss Reed's voice. "No, I'd sooner take my chances with the ship." She was being pulled along by two gentlemen to the windows. But there she balked. A crewman standing beside her tore an object from her hands and hurled it into the lifeboat. Howling in outrage, Miss Reed dived into the boat. Then I realized the object thrown was her "lucky" toy pig.

I heard a man say, "Room for more ladies in this boat," and I drew back. I could not go. I could only turn and bolt back to the warmth of the glowing ship.

My mind was numbed by cold and fear. But I knew then what I was doing. I could not remember that I hated Amanda Whitwell. It occurred to me that she would die. Perhaps we both would die. But if I lived and she did not, I couldn't have the burden on my conscience that she had been on my life. I raced to find her.

I had nearly reached the end of B corridor when a steward loomed up from nowhere. "Here now, you oughtn't to be down here!" He caught my arm to turn me back.

"Tell me where Mr. Sawyer's stateroom is," I said. "Please, I have to know!"

He spoke in a husky whisper. "Well, miss, I'll tell you the truth. But then you must promise to go."

At my nod, he took my hand and led me to a narrow

stairwell. As we stood at the top of a flight, he said, "I'm the steward for Mr. Sawyer's stateroom, miss. It was down on C deck."

"Was?" I said.

"Look down, miss."

At the bottom, black water lapped at the stairs. "Mr. Sawyer's stateroom is underwater, miss. Has been this past quarter hour."

I couldn't believe the greater part of the ship was dead already—I couldn't believe what my mind's eye saw: Miss Amanda lying trapped against the ceiling of a room, a death trap swirling to the top with freezing water—her hair, hair like mine, turned to a seaweed's tendrils. And here I stood a few feet away, dry-shod still. It couldn't be. And yet I knew it was.

Down the tilting corridor I ran, my mind oddly clear. I knew what I must do now. I must live. Whoever I was, whatever I had been, wherever I was going—I must live.

I rushed to Miss Amanda's stateroom. In the steamer trunk I found a fur-trimmed wrap, wadded with her other things. How flimsy the wrap looked as I threw it over my vest and tied its silken cord at my neck. I turned to the treasure on the dressing table. Diamond bracelets, a brooch, a pendant. The necklace of pearls. I snatched up the pearls and wound them around my neck, stuffing the end of the loop into my life preserver. Then the circle of gold set with an enormous diamond. I jammed it onto the finger that had once worn John Thorne's ring. This engagement ring and the pearls—these must be saved, for they were Mr. Forrest's gifts.

The lamps flickered and dimmed. My hair whipped

madly about my face as I fled. I ran toward music. Yes, the ship's orchestra still played—a lively ragtime tune. It pulled me on toward the grand staircase. But the steps pitched backward. They seemed to lead nowhere. But I leaped at them, fell, crawled up to the landing, and on up to A deck.

People were clustering at the rail, women and men, waiting. They cried out as a boat from the open deck above, teeming with people, began descending in fits and starts. Would it stop for them? It made no stop, but lowered quickly past their horrified gaze.

Then a man broke from the shadows and darted through the crowd. He leaped like a monkey onto the rail, hands and feet drawn together, and soared out into space, flinging himself down onto the heads of those in the lifeboat.

I ran back into the ship, across the foyer to the starboard side, and stepped up to the rail. A lifeboat was settling into the flat oil-stained sea below. When I looked up, I saw the davits on this side of the boat deck were all empty.

The ship shuddered and the hiss of steam ceased. Over the chorus of hundreds of far-off voices crying out, I heard music again, a mournful, stately melody now that broke as I listened, notes scattered to the wind.

The ship began to slide. It shook, and there were explosions deep within it. Boilers giving way, perhaps. Or the collapse of kitchen crockery. Or the great crystal chandeliers thundering down on parquet floors. The *Titanic*, her stern standing high out of the water, was sliding into the sea.

The water rose to meet me. I threw a leg over the rail and balanced there, watching the strange, rolling waterfall that surged beside the ship's hull. I was not six feet above it. I leaped out into the maelstrom, and the water's first icy blow knocked me senseless and stopped my breath.

I was drawn down, down below the rushing surface until the cork vest, bobbing upward, carried me with it. Suddenly my head broke the surface, and I saw the ship still making its slide into the blackness, its stern swarming with people. One of the great funnels buckled and fell into the water with a hard slap. I was thrust backward by the shock wave, thrust clear of the suction that dragged the other swimmers down.

There was no feeling in my hands and feet. But I had to move. I couldn't die by inches in this way—freezing in the act of drowning. But my soaked hair drew my face down, and the knot of silk cord at my neck combined with the necklace of pearls to close my throat. Lower and lower I was drawn, like a starfish caught in a whirlpool.

The pain in my arms to the elbows told me I wasn't quite helpless. And I swam, I flailed, I struggled through the water.

For how long? An hour—two? No, it couldn't have been more than five minutes. But I could have slept then, easily and forever, except one last urge grew within me. I thrust myself up for one last swallow of freezing air, and my skull seemed to splinter against some hard, unyielding object.

My hands grappled upward and found the solid wood of a board set just above the lapping waves. I managed to cling there and struggle for a better hold.

It was an airless place, under that narrow plank, stuffy and freezing and black as a pocket. I was in some enclosure and could hear the rumbling sound of men's boots and men's voices. They were somewhere just above me and the thing I clung to. I was neither alone nor dead. But where was I?

The heel of my hand worked down the curving wall to the waterline and then beneath it. There below the water I felt its lower edge. I ducked my head again beneath the surface and followed around the wooden lip that floated half in and half out of the sea.

The cork vest buoyed me suddenly upward and I was in open sea again. I had surfaced beneath an overturned lifeboat. The plank had been a seat stretched across the boat's midsection. Now I was clinging to the outer hull. And just above my face were the boots of a dozen men— perhaps more—standing on the overturned boat's curving underside. And there were others in the water, struggling toward us. Some cried out, "Save one life! Save one life!"

I held on to the boat's edge, my head so near that those standing above me, swaying back and forth on bending knees to keep the shell on an even keel, couldn't see me at first. I clung there, knowing I couldn't live long in this water, while the men above me moaned low in their throats. I took them for stokers who had escaped somehow from the furnace room and coal hole.

The sea was a black expanse now, as if the ship had never been. But then a man's head suddenly surfaced beyond the end of the boat. He threw up an arm and shouted. One of the men above me roared, "Get away!

Get away! You'll swamp us, you fool!" But the man in the water was no threat to them. His hand fell away, and I saw nothing more of him.

My hand crept along the overlapping planks of the hull. But I could do no more. And then I clutched the toe of a stoker's boot.

He jerked his foot away, and the boat wobbled crazily. "Get off, get off, you bleeding leech. I'll deal with you!"

He was wielding an oar. At the risk of his own balance, he swung it in an arc like a pendulum to sweep me away. The oar caught me full in the face, seeming to crush my cheekbone. I floated free then, pinwheels of pale lightning in my brain.

Then another voice. "My God. It's a woman!"

"Can't be," came another voice. Did they all have oars to beat me away from their refuge?

But then they were drawing me out of the water. "We're all but capsized," came a voice, "and for what? To bring another corpse aboard?"

No, I tried to cry, *no, I am not dead. Don't roll me off!* But I could only moan. It was enough, though. And I was left to lie across the lifeboat's keel.

All the cries from the water had ceased now. It would have been absolutely still if the men above me, braced against the swell of the sea, had not begun to pray. *"Yea, though I walk through the valley of the shadow of death . . ."* Then my mind slipped away, into deeper darkness.

I awoke to shouts, remembering nothing. The world had gone from black to gray. Hands grasped my body. I felt myself drawn over the keel and lifted into another lifeboat.

"Make room here," a woman's voice said. "Lay her across my knees." I heard a gasp. "Oh, dear Lord, don't look at her face!"

I felt my hands being taken and briskly massaged. Then a light touch at my neck felt for a pulse. "Look!" said the woman's voice. "Those pearls. It's Amanda Whitwell."

I lay there, still not quite knowing.

The pain crept back now, and one of my eyes was swollen shut. Each time I came near waking, the day was brighter. At last the world was suffused with rosy light. But the talk, the cries—all were meaningless to me. I lay cradled in pain and waited until I could understand the riddle, the puzzle of words I had heard when I was handed into this boat.

Hands clutched me. A great ship loomed high above us. I could only wonder how it came to be there. How could any ship find this scatter of drifting lifeboats in the corpse-strewn sea? But our little boat rocked and nestled like a tug against this great ship's hull.

A ladder came down—ropes with wooden steps between. I was being held up, and hands ran ropes beneath my arms, around my body. I began to rise. Ocean and sky spread limitless in every direction. Icebergs, great shadowless structures, littered the sea.

Hands reached for me and drew me into the ship. I thought of Jonah, safe in his whale. They laid me gently on a floor unbelievably flat and solid, and I was sickened with the steadiness. The pearls rattled against the hard deck.

"She's very far gone," a voice said.

I wore Miss Amanda's wrap, her pearls, the ring Mr. Forrest had pledged his future with. I even wore my young lady's cast-off nightgown. And in this first confusion I was mistaken for Amanda Whitwell. My mind tried to embrace this fact.

This had happened before—when John Thorne had seized me that dark night. But now my own mother would not know me. My face was a bruised pulp. With the only eye I had any vision in, I could see my own cheek, swollen to grotesque size. The jewelry, of course, marked me as Miss Amanda. But that was a mistake. I could put it right at once.

I tried to speak. But I couldn't. *I am Miranda Cooke,* I said to whoever was there. *No, Miranda Thorne.* But no sound came. Perhaps I did not will it enough.

I was carried on a litter into a stateroom. It wasn't the sort of place where I should be quartered, and I tried to tell them. But someone bent over me and said, "It *is* a miracle! Mademoiselle Whitwell has saved herself!" It was Victorine.

Another voice spoke. "Amanda?" Miss Rebecca Reed's hand touched me. "But where is her maid?"

Victorine whimpered. "I look and look all over this ship. I ask everyone. I look even under the blankets covering the dead. But there is no Miranda." She swallowed a sob. "Perhaps there will be another lifeboat?"

"They are all in now and accounted for, except those that were swamped," Miss Reed answered softly. "We can only pray for the others and wonder why we were chosen to live."

I drifted into sleep. But before I was quite unconscious, I heard Victorine say, "Then Miranda is dead." I seemed to hear it over and over until the voice became my own: "Miranda is dead."

The ship that had saved us was the *Carpathia*. It had been making its unhurried way from New York to the Mediterranean along a southern route. When the *Titanic* had sent out its frantic messages on that fatal night, the *Carpathia* alone had answered the call.

At dawn when it reached this nameless stretch of sea, its passengers could hardly believe their eyes: women, dressed in the height of fashion, rising directly from the sea; infants, blue with cold, lying in the arms of dumbstruck nurses. Mrs. Brown appeared on the deck, her hands a mass of broken blisters, for she'd pulled on the oars through the night. Mrs. Astor in her smart dress and smarter hat stared back in disbelief at the sea that had taken her husband. Mrs. Ryerson reached out again and again to embrace her three children, to still their questions about their father.

Seven hundred such survivors stumbled or were lifted into the *Carpathia*. And those found dead in the open boats were laid out with as much dignity as could be summoned. But the *Carpathia* only paused where the unsinkable ship had vanished. It lingered in a wash of deck chairs and debris and empty life jackets. It crept across the grave of the fifteen hundred lost, and then it steamed away.

Messages fanned out across the unbelieving world, a world that held its breath until the *Carpathia* sailed into New York harbor three days later.

I lay in the stateroom through those days as one who has died and waits to learn of an afterlife. I lay in the twilight world of the concussion victim, unable to speak. And then unwilling. A doctor reset a shoulder I didn't know was dislocated, and then my right arm lay useless in a sling across my breast. The doctor cleaned and bandaged my cheek and my forehead.

"Will she come back to herself?" A lady's voice asked him.

"Time will do what it can," he answered. "She will not be the same as before."

I wanted to agree. I wanted to meet the doctor's gaze, but I didn't dare. I, the helpless imposter, lay there pretending to sleep. I could find my voice, perhaps. But could I find the voice of Amanda Whitwell? I willed myself to sleep, withdrawing.

It was the evening of April 18 when we entered New York harbor. The tugboats lined us into land. And beyond was the sound of masses of people calling out, crying for the first word, calling out the names of the living and the dead. I couldn't go on like this. I must tell someone the truth. I managed to move the hand that was not in the sling. The diamond flashed. But then I lost the thread of my thought.

When I awoke, stretcher bearers were in the room.

Beside me, someone had taken my hand. His necktie was pulled loose. My hand and its ring were lost in his grasp. I turned toward him as toward the light. He bent his head over my hand. His hair was lustrous black. My heart turned over, and I passed a great barrier. It was Mr. Gregory Forrest, come to claim Miss Amanda Whitwell.

When next I awoke, I was in a hospital bed. New bandages throbbed at my cheek and at my temples, and stitches had been taken in my lip. But he was there, silent beside my bed. As the days dimmed and brightened in no particular order, I grew used to seeing him there.

Once, an elderly woman was in his place. Her hand covered mine, and she spoke to me as if I were her own child. I seemed to know that this was Gregory Forrest's mother.

I heard a doctor say, "She should be clearing now. There is no reason why she shouldn't begin to speak soon. And to understand."

But there were reasons—enormous reasons. I was not who they thought me to be.

Gregory Forrest asked the doctor, "Is it possible that she will never be . . . well?"

"Time is the great healer," the doctor said, easing away from an answer. "We do not foresee permanent damage to mind or body. But she may not be quite as she was before."

I clung to those words, finding my future in them. "Not quite as she was before." I was ready to follow the path that seemed to open before me.

He was sitting by my bed again. He had been there every day, keeping a morning watch before he went off to his work. I had loved him for so long that it didn't seem strange. I remembered meeting him in the great hallway of Whitwell Hall, where I'd blundered in my maid's uniform. He had asked me my name, and I remembered Lady Eleanor's footfall on the stairs that had sent me scurrying down the servants' steps. I remembered the throb beneath the heart that only he inspired.

"Amanda?" he said, and I dared not stir in the hospital bed.

"Yes?" I said through broken lips. "Yes."

I was removed from the hospital to Gregory Forrest's family home in Brooklyn, to a room more comforting than any I had ever known. It wasn't as grand as Whitwell Hall, but it was spacious and more homelike than lavender silks.

There was also a saucy little flaxen-haired maid of all work named Ursula, who served me now with a breezy independence. Once I dared speak at all, I asked her to bring me a mirror.

Ursula hesitated. "Mrs. Forrest said you wasn't supposed to see yourself. But Lord have mercy, you look so much better than you did. . . . Maybe just a peek. But you mustn't start yellin' and carryin' on."

I must have looked very startled and ladylike at that, for Ursula grinned and brought me a hand mirror. I put my uninjured hand out with some of the impatience of Amanda Whitwell. Ursula hovered, worrying, as I stared into a face that was neither mine nor Amanda Whitwell's. I took more comfort in what I saw than Ursula could know.

It was the face of a battered stranger. My eyes were swollen. My cheek and my eyebrows were crisscrossed with lines that had recently been an angry red. I looked at a thin line of scar tissue that broke the arch of my right eyebrow, and I recalled that Miss Amanda's eyebrow had been divided in just such a way from a long-ago fall from a horse. By now I had come past the time for telling the truth. I was becoming Amanda Whitwell. I looked into the violet eyes, shaded by pain and the vagueness of concussion. Those too could pass as Amanda's. She seemed to be alive there within the mirror, behind the eyes. I saw the schemer that she had been in those eyes, and then I remembered they were mine.

A letter lay on the bedside table one morning. The stamp was British and the spidery, perfect handwriting was Lady Eleanor Whitwell's. Now I must take up another thread of a life that wasn't mine:

My darling daughter,

Your father and I thank God that your life has been spared. The anguish of uncertainty is behind us now, and I only pray that you are all but restored to health. I place my trust in Gregory.

I think often of the many opportunities you and I have lost in the past to be truly mother and daughter. I can only hope that when you are a married woman, however far away, you and I will find a way to grow closer, if only in our thoughts.

In the midst of our rejoicing at your survival, the household has been saddened by the loss of your maid and good companion, Miranda. We pray for her soul. Your father has informed John Thorne of the death of his wife. . . .

I wept not as the daughter of such a loving mother, but as one who has never known such love. I wept too for the Miranda who was dead now, dead and remembered with kindness.

Ursula, who never knocked, found me crying. She ran to find Mrs. Forrest, who came and hovered at the door until I asked her to sit beside me. I couldn't put her off. I could no longer keep those willing to love me at arm's length.

"You are . . . moved, perhaps, by a vord from your home?"

I nodded and tried to smile.

"I understand such a thing." Her eyes grew bright with the hint of tears. Gregory had her eyes. "I came from the Old Country, from Augsburg, ven I vas no more than a girl. And since, I have shed my share of tears over letters from home, though this has been my happy home for more years than you have lived. It is your mother who sends you vord?"

I nodded again.

"And there are others besides your mother and papa? A grandmother, perhaps?"

"No," I said, struggling to turn my lies into a kind of truth. "There is a very old woman, though, with a heart full of love. She lives in a cottage on . . . our grounds. She has been like a . . . grandmother to me. She's had many hardships, but she has made her memories happy, as I hope to make mine."

Mrs. Forrest patted the back of my hand, and I turned it to hold hers. She began to talk, to reminisce. She spoke of her husband and his rise to prosperity; of the hopes and plans of her son. She told me about these men she loved, and I heard more of Gregory Forrest than Amanda Whitwell ever had.

In the evenings Gregory himself sat beside my bed. In those evenings the Amanda he had loved began to interweave with the Amanda before him. He had fallen in love with an image I could not hope to match. I could not stun him with my wit or raise a satirical eyebrow while I dangled him on a string. I could only hope to be more loving and more kind, a better wife to him than Amanda would have been.

At first I contented myself with being an eager listener. But there was so much I wanted to know. And one evening I spoke to him as soon as he was beside me. I gripped his hand to screw up my courage. "Gregory, I feel very foolish and very forgetful." Yes, that was spoken in one of Miss Amanda's more languid tones, though it lacked her utter boredom. "Your mother has been good enough to sit with me—"

"And talk you into a trance about her son's boyhood?" he said.

"Well, she did just touch on the subject in passing."

He squeezed my hand. "And what do you want to know that Mother didn't get around to telling you?"

"It's serious, Gregory. Your mother spoke of your father, and I don't know if he is . . . living."

"No, my dearest. My father died very suddenly not long after I met you."

I seemed to stand at the edge of quicksand. "Oh, Gregory, I must have known, mustn't I?"

"No, my dear, you wouldn't have known. It happened at one of those times when you had—well, you'd banished me. Then when we were together again, I didn't want to trouble you."

"Gregory, there is *nothing* now that I don't want to know. Nothing that concerns you can fail to concern me. I've been very tiresome and childish in the past."

I listened as he told me of his work, his family, his boyhood friend Sammy Bettendorf, who had died needlessly in a firetrap tenement. He told me what had given him the goals that directed his life, and I was scarcely able to hope that I could play my role at his side. I would have been drawn by his selfless ambitions even if I had not loved him.

He opened his heart through the evening that stretched almost till dawn. Then he drew me up short. "But you've heard all this before, Amanda. All my schemes to rebuild New York as a place fit for people to live in safety and dignity."

"I could hear it many more times, Gregory."

"And you no longer think—let's see, how did you put it once—that I 'reek of idealism'?"

"I could never have said such a thing!" I replied, in absolute honesty.

Then Gregory was beside me on the bed. His arms moved gently but confidently around me and held me in his sheltering embrace. He didn't yet attempt to kiss my bruised face, for that might have given me pain. But I felt pain, and doubt, at what I had set in motion. My lies had been only too successful. I sank out of my depth, tormented by fear. And there would be more deceit. More than even that other Amanda had ever needed. Was any love worth this eternity of lies?

I knew it was. I knew it was worth anything. I'd never demanded anything of life before. But I was not now what

I had been. I forced myself to lie easily in his embrace, and I held him as tightly as one hand could manage.

"You are all I want," he said. And all the world beyond us fell away.

Gregory Forrest and I were married in June 1912. My only attendant was Miss Rebecca Reed.

She had left her card at the Forrest home in Bushwick sometime before, and I'd been thrown into a panic. Here was a keen-eyed woman who had known both Amanda and me well enough to notice our similarities, and our differences. I would not see her, and she had to make the long trip back to Manhattan with only coffee and the apologies of Gregory's mother.

But much as I wanted to, I could not hide from the world forever. My arm was out of the sling, so I wrote Rebecca Reed a note, pleading bad health and asking her back another afternoon.

Delighted with this evidence of my recovery, Mrs. Forrest ordered from Abraham & Straus a tea gown with all possible accessories. On the day of the visit, I dressed my hair precisely as I had dressed Amanda Whitwell's. I spent the final moments moving through a ritual by rote that I had before practiced on another. Ursula opened the front door below, and I hung there on the long staircase a moment longer. My hand gripped a banister of black walnut, but there was nothing to be done about my pounding heart. I started down the stairs.

Mrs. Forrest had already burdened Miss Reed with coffee and a plate of cakes by the time I appeared in the parlor doorway. I forced myself to greet her by her first name and to move across the room in the posture of a lady. I had worried that my face and my speech would undo me. Now I feared that my carriage, and the mannerisms of a servant, would betray me first.

Miss Reed searched my face with a reporter's professional intensity. "My dear Amanda, you're very nearly perfection again! How lucky for you—and for us all."

I was just able to meet her look, and I urged her to tell Mrs. Forrest the story of her musical pig, the sole story from the great horror that might be told over coffee to amuse. Miss Reed was a natural storyteller, and I sat, smiling and nodding, easing by degrees into the chair. If only I could let the rest of the world do the talking, perhaps it would save the moment, and my life.

At last, when I thought Miss Reed meant to rise and go, she turned to me and set her cup aside. "You know, Amanda, journalists are outrageously thick-skinned types. We have to be if we mean to make a living. What I'm trying to say is this: Would it be too painful for you to give me an interview about your experience on the *Titanic*? You see, the New York papers are still yearning for every inch of copy they can get. And frankly, I'd like to write an account from your viewpoint. I know, I know, you really shouldn't have to relive the whole terrible business." She waved a hand as if to dismiss herself. But then she fixed me with a very direct, perhaps calculating look.

I drew back from the idea of an interview. Every word I spoke of a life that was not mine might trip me up. But I knew I must grant her an interview, before she found the fear in my eyes. For the rest of my life, however I might live it, I would be recalled as a survivor of this famous disaster. That I would never escape. Perhaps a word now would forestall many later.

When Mrs. Forrest saw I was willing to be interviewed, she left us, only warning Miss Reed not to "question me to death." When we were alone, Rebecca Reed drew her chair closer. *If she knows,* I thought, *this will be her opportunity to accuse me.* But no, she was merely flipping open her notepad, poising her pen. Oh how I yearned to rise up at this woman and scream, I AM NOT AMANDA WHITWELL. If you know it, don't torture me anymore. And if you hadn't known till now, keep my guilty secret, for I have no other life to live but hers. . . .

And yet I sat so silently, fingering my pearls. I appeared to be forcing myself to remember moments that were only painful and not damning.

"There are things," I said in a thoughtful, distant voice, "that I don't recall at all. The shock perhaps. And it had been such an ordinary evening. Dinner and coffee, and afterwards a turn on the deck. Yes, I'm quite sure of that much. I wore my pink. And the silver slippers."

"You weren't alone, surely," Miss Reed said, watching.

"No, I strolled the deck with Mr. Sawyer."

That was true enough. I'd seen them. But had they dined together, taken their coffee together in the Palm Court? Had Miss Reed seen them?

But she only said, "And then?"

"I went to . . . my stateroom and went to bed rather early."

Rebecca Reed's pen hovered above the page. Discretion and the dictates of journalism battled within her.

"Rebecca," I said, "I realize that some of the passengers misunderstood my friendship with Mr. Sawyer. I had flirted outrageously with him. Yet, as shipboard ro-

mances go, ours was an innocent flirtation. But it did oc-
cur to me that perhaps Mr. Sawyer's reputation as a . . .
lady-killer had preceded him. I sent him away early on
that Sunday night, and I never saw him again."

There. I couldn't avoid mentioning Clem Sawyer. He
hung heavily in Rebecca Reed's mind. Ironically, I was being more careful of Miss Amanda's reputation than she
herself had ever been. But the interview was far from over.

"You were awakened by the sound of the ship striking the iceberg?"

"No. My . . . maid awakened me."

"Oh!" Miss Reed cried, "I'm so glad to know you
don't claim to have heard the first impact of ship against
iceberg! Half the people interviewed said it sounded like
a thunderclap. What rot! It was quite a small sound."

"I sent Miranda to the purser for my jewelry. Then I
simply went back to sleep. It seems very foolish now.

"I awoke again some while later. The stateroom stood
at an alarming angle. Miranda and I threw on life preservers. I reached for my jewelry, and we went out to see
what was happening." I stopped, fearful of the sound of
my own voice, wondering how I could continue this
awful mingling of truth and falsehood.

Miss Reed busied herself with her notes, saying,
"Surely there was still time to get yourselves into a
lifeboat?"

"The deck was a . . . terrific muddle. I was frightened,
and I'm sorry to say I gave way to an unreasonable in-
stinct. I rushed back to my stateroom to get a book, a diary that I kept. Perhaps it seemed a memento—rather
like your pig. I . . . never saw Miranda again."

"Yes," Miss Reed said thoughtfully. "People did go back for the most extraordinary things. And of course you weren't able to keep your diary with you. You must feel robbed of your past without it."

"I suppose I do," I said. And then I told her of my own salvation just as it had happened. I hoped the truth of this last part of my story would carry the falsehood of the first. I'd done my best and my worst.

When Miss Reed rose to go, I saw her to the door. "I hope," she said uncertainly, "that we can be friends. I feel I didn't know you before. I had quite the wrong impression of you."

All her crisp, professional manner fell away, and I wondered if I should take her hand. I said, "Everything is very strange in this new country. I shall depend upon my friends."

She hesitated. "You're feeling . . . well now?" How carefully she asked, more carefully than she needed to. I nodded, and as if she had said too much, she left quickly.

I stood for a long time behind the closed door. I could not decide if I had passed the test or failed it. Or if it had been a test at all. Surely it had gone well. But in that last moment. . . .

Perhaps she knew that Amanda Whitwell had been expecting a child. Could she think I might have lost the child in the sea? Perhaps she suspected the truth. Perhaps she knew I was an insignificant maid pathetically got up to impersonate a lady. Or did she, after all, see only that lady? I was never to know. The mercy of a stranger may well be the most valuable of all gifts and the least understood. Perhaps I posed such a great problem to

146

Rebecca Reed's determined open-mindedness that she could not solve me.

I stood before the looking glass in my bedroom on the night before I was to marry Gregory Forrest. The floor around me was awash in tissue paper and open boxes. My trousseau had arrived, sent by Lady Eleanor, from all the smartest shops in London. She had replaced the lost original trousseau down to the last detail. What pleasure it must have given her, this celebration of her daughter's survival.

I had always lined Miss Amanda's cast-off shoes with a bit of paper, for her feet were a size larger than my own. I bent now to layer paper into the butter-soft blue calf-skin shoes that I would wear when I wed the husband meant for her.

Then I thought of a scrap of verse: *"Something borrowed, something blue . . . and a penny for her shoe. . . ."* Suddenly the quiet, cluttered room filled with a distant voice. I froze, fearing it was Amanda's. But it was another, an older one. The Wisewoman's voice, as clear as on the day she'd foretold my fortune. The prophecy rang out again. And just as the Wisewoman had decreed, I'd died and come to life again beyond a mountain of ice.

She'd given me a gift—an American Indianhead penny—and told me to take it back, back where it had come from. She'd known my fate would lead me here. I had to find it. And yes, the gold chain that Gregory had given me. The chain that might betray and reveal me. My hand moved to my neck, where once the chain had lain hidden beneath the high collars of my servants' shirtwaist. But of course the chain was gone. It must have been lost in the sea. I would simply find another penny, one to honor the bridal traditions. In a small drawer of the dresser, where a few coins lay scattered, I found another Indianhead penny and slipped it into my shoe.

A soft knock at the door, and Gregory stepped into the room. I turned and rushed into his arms, and he held me until I stopped trembling.

"Better now?" he said at last, sheltering me from fears he would not ask me about.

"Much better."

"And better still tomorrow."

I could only nod at that.

The next afternoon we were married in a little Brooklyn church that would have been more at home in a field on the Isle of Wight. The four of us: Gregory and I, Mrs. Forrest, and Rebecca Reed clustered before the vicar. Sir Timothy had fallen ill, so there could be no thought of the Whitwells coming to America for the wedding.

When the vicar asked if anyone knew of any impediment to our union, my heart stopped. Yet no stranger stepped from the shadows to sever the knot now being tied. I heard Gregory's voice saying, "With this ring I thee wed." My hand was in his, and he placed there a gold band. The church walls did not split wide and dash me to death.

But with the word and the deed of this simple ceremony, I had become a criminal. A bigamist. I had married the only man in the world I could ever love. Yet I was married already, and to quite a different man.

Gregory and I were at home in our new house on Montague Terrace in Brooklyn from the first day of our marriage. We lived then, like all honeymooners, to love and to forget for a little time all the darkened world beyond the glow of our love.

It was an old house in a row of brick merchants' mansions, which Gregory, with an architect's skill and a husband's devotion, had made more modern and welcoming than its neighbors. The facade was repaved in limestone, silver gray, and Gregory added long windows that drew in the sun. The darker corners were lit by Tiffany lamps with shades like lily pads in silver and pale green to echo the walls. It was a house that invited joy and banished shadows. It spoke of the present, not the past.

From our back garden we looked directly out onto busy New York harbor. In the distance the Statue of Liberty raised her torch. In those star-filled summer nights great steamships began their voyages back to the world from which I'd come.

Our bedroom too looked out on this shifting scene. I stood before one of the windows on our wedding night, and the hand that bore its new wedding band grew cold with memory of that other band it had worn. And my other hand had signed two church registries, two marriage licenses within this single year.

Gregory stepped up behind me. I clung to his hands encircling my waist. I rested my head against his broad shoulder. I was in his arms, but my lies were between us. He kissed me more gently than I had ever been kissed before. But I had to speak, and now.

"I don't come to you as a bride should come to her husband. I am not—"

He turned me in his arms and his lips stopped my whispered confession. Then he said, "You come to me just as you are. You have come back almost from the dead. Our life begins now, with that miracle. Nothing before has ever happened."

We gave our first at-home party, a supper and dance, in that beautiful house on June 28. I stood beside Gregory at the door, and we greeted the arrivals without the intervention of a butler. I feared Gregory's friends, what they might see in me. But I fell back on the shyness of a new bride, smiling and nodding, accepting the inevitable compliments. I willed myself to believe that all of life would be so perfect.

My dancing was not noticeably worse than that of most of my admiring partners, and I marveled at the overwhelming friendliness of Americans. They were determined to make me welcome. If I had possessed the meanest Cockney accent, they would have thought it charming. Having been told my father was a knight, they treated me with hearty deference. They left me with the fleeting impression that I could do no wrong. Every woman deserves one such night, whatever price she must pay in the morning.

The next afternoon the house still bore the signs of a successful party. Mrs. Forrest had lent me Ursula until I had time to engage my own staff. She was down in the kitchen, trying to create order there. I was alone and very much myself, performing the duties of a parlormaid.

The front doorbell rang. Tearing off my apron, I fled up to my room to return myself to some version of a leisured lady. I stepped quickly out of my cotton dress and into a tea gown. Just as I was easing into a pair of slippers, Ursula appeared in my room.

"There's a man here to see you, Mrs. Forrest. Says he knows you and says he has something to deliver. But he isn't wearing a uniform or nothin' like that."

No, he wouldn't be, I thought. "His name?"

Ursula had forgotten to ask. But it didn't matter. I knew who he was. "Show him into the front hall, Ursula. I'll be down in a moment."

In that moment I rushed to the front of the house to look down on the street. My throat closed as it had closed in the sea when I saw what stood at our door, already attracting a crowd of small boys. It was a Rolls-Royce limousine, immensely long and high, all its brightwork mirroring the sunlight. If it had been a hearse sent to bear my dead body away, I could not have felt more lost. I wished it were a hearse, come for me.

I stood at the head of the stairs as long as I dared. Long enough to know that he was standing in the hallway below. I saw the flaxen lights in his hair, alive in the dim light. I saw his heavy arms slung down at his sides, the breadth of his shoulders beneath the straining serge of the dark suit he had worn at our marriage. I began to walk down the stairs in a gown suddenly too fine. I walked blind with fear and empty of any idea. I did not know what he expected. I only knew that he was John Thorne. The only man to whom I was legally bound. My husband.

He turned and his eyes moved upward, from my slippered toe to the draped silk of my skirt to the sash at my waist. At last to my eyes. Then he moved toward me, and I put up a hand, glancing toward the back stairs. It was as imperious a gesture as Miss Amanda's. Perhaps it *was* hers. I nodded toward the front drawing room, and he stepped back to let me lead him there. Would he have done the same for Miranda?

I had hardly gone beyond the entrance to the room before his rough hands seized my waist. I whirled on him. "No!" I muttered and flung his hands away. I told him to sit, and I took up a position beside the mantel.

When he spoke, his voice startled me. I'd forgotten the country burr. And I'd forgotten the heavy animal strength in his body, the weather-whipped face, the hands. . . .

"So you have nothing for me, then?" It was a soft growl, threatening, perhaps, only because I thought so.

"What is it you want?" I tried to read his eyes and couldn't. Yet he watched me—her—like hunter's prey, new light showing in those unexpressive eyes.

"Well, if there's no chance of more privacy than what we've got now, a kiss, perhaps."

"I think not." Would he spring on me? I knew what he had had from her. How could Amanda Whitwell, so free with herself before, stand on her dignity now?

But he was only turning a tweed cap in his hands. A sweat-stained chauffeur's cap that spoke more eloquently than either of us.

"I've brought the Rolls-Royce, Sir Timothy's gift. 'Twill show the Yanks a thing or two about what a proper automobile is all about."

The words didn't match the faintly thoughtful tone of his voice. He looked down at the cap in his hand. He was not the sullen rebel or the handsome brute, but more the servant than I remembered.

"Whatever we had planned," I began, "must be considered again. Things that seemed possible when—"

"She was alive," he interrupted. And I remained quiet, not knowing how I had meant to finish. "Things look different nearer to," he said, and he ceased looking at me altogether. He'd looked his fill. He stared at the rug at my feet. "You're—content here, then?"

"Yes. More content than I had thought to be."

"And want for nothing more?"

"No. Nothing."

He gripped his cap as if he would turn it inside out. "And yet a long, hard time I've had coming here," he said.

"Not so hard a time as I," I retorted with the spirit of both Amanda and Miranda combining.

"No," he said. "Two weeks on an old tub out of Liverpool for me. But you fared far worse. There in the first days we thought—we feared you were both dead."

"And if Miranda had lived and I had died . . ."

His gazed stopped me. "Miranda did live," he said. "Amanda died."

The stillness of the afternoon dropped like a shroud.

"You knew," I said finally.

"I know now. I didn't know before. When Sir Timothy told me my wife was dead in the sea, I believed him. Had no reason not to. I've always taken my betters at their word. You have reason to know that. I'm in this room now on the far side of the world because I've followed the ghost of a dead woman who'd bewitched me. But you're that woman now. And you want nothing from me."

"I want more from you than ever she did," I said.

"Yes, but it will not be so easy to grant."

We both pondered that. I was not one of his betters who might command him and he obey out of habit. He who had always lived in their thrall knew an impostor when he saw one. It would do me no good to turn on him now like a cornered vixen.

"It's easy to see how they think—they think you're her."

"And yet you weren't fooled."

"No." He looked away, seeming to spare me, seeming not to take notice of my stylish hair, my expensive gown.

"What gives me away? Not that it can still matter."

"There's not the calculation in your eye."

"Oh, but there is. I've done nothing but scheme and plot and lie. I almost dare not open my mouth for fear I'll tell the truth, or that the truth will tell itself."

"Ah, but it's from need," John said. "*She* calculated and connived because it was her nature. I don't speak ill of the dead. It was her nature. She was mad, and you're not."

"And yet you mourn her loss," I said.

"No, lass. I mourn yours."

The stillness descended again. He mourned me as I stood before him, yearning to live. John Thorne mourned me, and I could not grasp his meaning.

"I am your wife." I had to force myself to say it. "And I have married another man, whom I love. I had never known real love before, and neither had he. But that is no excuse. The marriage is not legal. You are the only person who knows the truth. You must do with it what you will. If you take from me now what I have, at least I will keep the memory of it. I will not even hate you, if I can help it."

He sat slumped in the chair, immensely weary. The strength seemed to drain from him. But he looked more a man, slumped there, than he had ever looked before. "You had as much right to marry Forrest as I had to marry you."

"And what do we make of those two wrongs?" I believe even now that I would have agreed to anything he asked. I was wearier than he.

"Perhaps we make a pact."

"The last woman you entered into a pact with—"

"Is dead," he said in a hoarse whisper. "I would claim you if I could. But I claimed you before only to let you be used, and so I won't claim you now."

I stood motionless, not yet able to feel the warmth in this faint ray of hope.

"I took you because you were like her. . . . Would you believe me if I told you that in those few weeks we lived as man and wife, I began to think for myself? I began to know you were the better woman, and better for me? But it was too late."

"If you had a genuine feeling for me, it will not make things easier for us now," I said.

"Ah, the paths you and I set out on were never meant to be easy, were they?"

I waited. The afternoon light slanted lower in the room. My hus—Gregory would soon be home. But still, John and I must play out our hands. There was no other way.

When I looked up again, he was standing. His cap hung from his hand, but he did not twirl it like some bumpkin underling. "I'll leave you to him. You deserve a fresh start—a real chance at a life for yourself. I'll make no demands on you. You're dead to those who knew us both. And you'll be to your husband what . . . *she* couldn't have been. You'll have his child one day, and not mine." His eyes flickered down to my narrow waist. He had seen that narrowness in his first glance, as I stood on the stairs.

"But still, we are married."

"No," he said. "I'm a widower, and the few who know me know that."

"You'll go back to the Isle?"

He looked up in surprise. "What's there for me in England? No, I'll see a bit of this country, where it's said a man can make his own way. I'll go west and farm or hunt or hire out by the day." I saw the far distances in his eyes. "By the day," he repeated, "not the night."

He was turning to go, dissolving the last link between us. The fear that had dogged me began to fade. I was left with an emotion that was neither joy nor despair. And I couldn't let him go without saying what was in my heart.

"Because of today," I said, "I shall never think of you with bitterness. I shall remember you—fondly—for the rest of my life."

He stopped, his back to me. His head dipped low. He was not a man capable of tears, I thought. And yet I shall never be quite sure. I walked behind him to the door. He slung his cap on his head.

"The Rolls," I said. It gleamed at the curb, and he reached in his pocket for the keys. "No," I said. "You keep it. Take it."

He turned then, the ghost of a smile playing at his mouth. His eyes crinkled. Had I ever seen him smile before? "You've come a long way, lass, if you're handing out Rolls-Royces to strange men who come to your door." It was the only jest John Thorne and I ever shared.

"No," he said, "I'll make my way in this new country on my own feet. It's a hulking great thing anyhow, that Rolls, and not much use on rough roads." He dropped the keys into my hand and walked away. Our fingers never touched.

I watched him stride to the corner. The evening sun was bright on his back. He squared his shoulders as he went. It was a gesture I could understand. He walked in a new posture, in a new land. We had that in common. I watched him out of sight, and the tears coursed down my cheeks. Tears of joy and loss and redemption and whatever else tears are made of.

I had been Mrs. Gregory Forrest for more than a year. And by a husband's love I was transformed far beyond my desperate attempts to transform myself. His was a world of unfurling blueprints. It was the clean smell of new lumber and fresh paint when he returned from a building site. He was inflamed and often exhausted by his work. I shared it. Our hopes together went into the bricks and steel that rose against the sky.

Montague Terrace
November 4, 1913

My dearest Mother and Father,

If my letters have said too little over the past months, it was only to give me the pleasure of breaking happy news with some attempt at flair. On the night before last, you became grandparents.

A little grandson, with all his fingers and toes intact, and eyes a startling blue. Gregory believes they will shade to violet in time, to honor his mother.

Gregory and I have not decided on a name. But I imagine we will settle on Theodore—Ted—an American President's name, for the first member of the Whitwell line to be American by birth.

We are all three very happy. His proud father has done over the sunniest room as the nursery, so Baby will have quite a proper suite.

I am sorry, Father, that your health doesn't permit an ocean voyage, for I would very much like to see you with your grandson on your knee. But we shall have a trip home to Whitwell Hall as soon as Baby is old enough to be a good traveler. To share this news with you, dear Mother and Father, adds to the joy I feel today.

Your devoted
Amanda

The real Amanda would not have found much joy in Gregory's world. I can't believe she would have flourished in the warmth of his love as I did. And her child would not have been his, as mine was. Still, I felt the silent thrusts of guilt. That guilt was the impulse behind the letters I wrote regularly to Lady Eleanor and Sir Timothy. I composed them with great care, reaching for scraps of memory to make a changed but believable daughter. For I wanted Lady Eleanor to experience the love she deserved.

Yet I often lied in those letters, showing an eagerness to visit England that I didn't feel. But I did not have to think of an excuse to postpone such a visit. In August of 1914 the Great War thundered out of the Balkans and erupted over Europe.

Then in May of 1915 America lurched nearer the war with the sinking of the British liner *Lusitania*. The country began to mobilize. I closed the curtains of our long front windows as the harbor of New York grew steadily more congested with ships painted a dull gray. Like so many wives, I saw the war cast a shadow across my husband's face. He became preoccupied with that distant threat, and I longed to think he was past the age for soldiering. But I couldn't be sure. At the darkest edges of my mind I saw him already dead in some foreign trench even before I saw him in a uniform.

In 1917 America entered the war. Gregory was commissioned captain in the army engineers. We had been married for five years. I felt my world shudder to a halt.

He was sent overseas in early autumn. During his last leave, his military boots, polished to glass, stood like sentinels in our room. All the brusque, mystical world of warring men invaded our house, so that even in those few days together we were not alone. But on the night before Gregory was to go, we stood together in the shadows of the nursery until Teddy drifted off to sleep. I stood very near his father, and in the faint glow of the night-light we both gazed down at our son's dark curls against the pillow, trying to extend that moment to eternity.

We had a late supper on trays before the living-room hearth. The curtains were drawn, and the only light came from the flames. As we sat before the fire, I lay within Gregory's arms. The quiet and the nearness should have been enough. But I knew I could not let him go without telling him the truth. Surely it had been all the lies of the world that had brought civilization to this brink. My brave smiles in seeing my husband off to war were falsehood enough. I must clear my conscience of an older deceit, and a greater one.

When he sensed I was about to speak, his arms moved closer around me. But I could say nothing. I only closed my hands over his. He spoke instead. "What we have to do now will be a small enough price to pay for the five years of happiness we've had."

I nodded, my eyes brimming.

"Have these years been as happy for you as they've been for me?"

"They have been the whole of my life," I said.

"And there'll be many more years after the war."

"Gregory, when I say that our time together has been the whole of my life, I mean it literally. Before we were married, before in England, I was a stranger to you."

"Two people are always strangers before they're married. Friends rarely marry."

"But few are ever such strangers as you and I were, Gregory."

He waited, and his hands tensed beneath mine.

"We had scarcely even met before—before I came to America."

Silence again, while he waited to hear me out. My head pitched forward. My shoulders drew in as I shuddered with every kind of fear. "Gregory, the young woman you fell in love with died in the sea. I'm not Amanda. I'm only her—"

Our fingers laced together. He drew me back to him. "You are everything I wanted in her," he said, "and more."

The fire crackled, throwing a fan of sparks against the screen. "You've known," I said, but he seemed not to hear.

"A man is capable of falling in love any number of times," he was saying. "Once I fell in love with a beautiful young vixen in a London drawing room who well knew how to make a young man suffer. Later I fell in love all over again, with a young woman lying very battered and very frightened in a hospital bed. Oh, I won't say I saw through her at once."

He loosed his hand from mine and slipped it into a pocket of his coat. "The day I brought you home from the hospital a nurse gave me your possessions, and among them was this." He drew out of his pocket a slender gold chain. It gleamed in the firelight, swaying there before my eyes. And from it dangled an Indianhead penny. The Wisewoman's coin.

"But I loved that girl in the hospital bed from the beginning, at first maybe because she needed it. Now I have other reasons. Each day I find a new one."

The tears streamed down my face. I mourned for all the time I had spent—had misspent—in playing a role that had failed. Yet the tears were of relief too, for the role had become real, and in that it was no failure.

"And still you never told me," I managed to say.

"Should I have?" Gregory asked. "It was your story—to tell or to keep. And if the past was painful for you, I wanted you to deal with it in your own way. After a while I rarely thought of it, though I think I knew all along that this evening would come."

"But, Gregory, there's more. I wasn't free to marry you. There's more you don't know."

"Don't I?" His arms cradled me with certainty. "Are you going to tell me that we have no marriage—that it doesn't exist? With our child asleep upstairs and all the world brandishing swords outside these walls, are you going to tell me we aren't married?"

His voice had fallen to a husky whisper. "No," I whispered back. "I couldn't tell you that. It wouldn't be true."

In June of 1918, precisely three quarters of a year after that evening, I gave birth to our second child, a fair-skinned, flashing-eyed little daughter I named Eleanor. But her father didn't hold her in his arms until she was six months old. And it was the most glorious Christmas of our lives, the Christmas after the war. We wept and we sang. The world was new-washed with freedom and peace and promise. And when my husband came home to me, I could not question the miracle. I could only hold him in wonder at his wholeness, looking beyond the lines the war had etched in his face.

The four of us made the much-postponed trip back to England in the summer of 1920. Sir Timothy had died in the first winter of peacetime. Lady Eleanor's letters had a faded, forgetful quality in them now. She was growing older, and she longed to know the grandchildren she had never seen. This journey was the last test of my credibility as the woman who had once been Amanda Whitwell. But I was resigned to confessing the truth to the one person left who deserved my honesty.

We sailed from New York on the *Olympic,* sister ship of the *Titanic.* I dreaded the voyage, and the sea. But aboard ship the mother of two small, active children has little time to indulge the ghosts of her memories. Although we included the nanny, Miss MacIntosh, in our party, by the time we disembarked at Southampton, both Eleanor and Teddy had reached the outer limits of their patience with traveling.

It was on the last leg of the journey, on the little train that ran across the Isle of Wight from Ryde to Shanklin, that I made myself remember this place that had once been all the world to me. The lonely cottages so like the Wisewoman's. The huts so like the one where my own parents—Mary Cooke's parents—might still be living. I gazed out of the train window while Gregory sat with his hand over mine, offering his strength in whatever role I was to play at Whitwell Hall, as the daughter of the house.

At Shanklin station, a beardless, stringy boy—too young to have died in the war—met us with a car hired for the occasion.

Here was the first ghost laid, for no rugged chauffeur steered a family limousine. I turned in relief to find Gregory's eyes on me, and I knew he followed my every thought.

It was evening when we drove up the avenue of black Italian pines and stopped beneath the portico of

Whitwell Hall. We stood there in our jumble of luggage, our two small children staggering in fatigue, clinging to Miss MacIntosh. When at last the door slowly opened, an elderly man stood there in a familiar coat grown loose on his frame. He was—what had *she* once said? "Quite as gray as an old rat." It was Mr. Finley—Finley.

His eyes had grown watery, imprecise; his movements slow and painful. Yet there was a whisper of the old authority in his shoulders and a hint of pride that must speak now of his being the only man of the house.

"Miss Amanda," he said. "It's Miss Amanda come home to us."

Lady Eleanor used a cane now. Her beauty, grown nearly transparent, echoed an earlier time. The choker of pearls at her neck called back to her Edwardian heyday and hid what time had put there since. I'd schooled myself over and over to call her Mother. Yet in that first moment we could only embrace. I buried my face that might betray me too soon against her shoulder as we held each other. I must be for her what she most wanted me to be.

But soon she had put me aside for a first look at the children, who were awed at the sight of this lady. She was a study in silver and pale blue, leaning on her silver-mounted cane. She led them inside and sat down at once to have small Eleanor in her lap and Teddy at her side. If their father and I had crept away in the twilight, we would not have been missed.

I had braced myself against Lady Eleanor's memories. But in her conversation she did not often draw us back to the days of the other Amanda. The war and time and the children stood between us and then. She was content to sit with me or the children. Often the only sound was the clinking of the tea things. I drank from cups I had never used, but their pattern was familiar, for I had washed them often enough.

And so, as those deep-summer days unfolded, I grew almost easy there. I awoke each morning to a world vivid with birdsong in the room where once I had brought in an early-morning tea tray. In the room where I had once found John Thorne beside Amanda Whitwell. Little about that room had changed, though the lavender hangings were paler now. But I had changed enough to sleep peacefully there with my husband at my side. As the passing days made me braver, I even dared explore the house and the grounds in the early-morning hours.

War had taken its toll, and taxes—later—would take the rest. I walked the grounds more freely than I had ever dreamed I could. For I knew this place would never be mine. When it was left to me, I knew that I would sell it. So I looked at it with the intensity of one who knew she would never see it again.

The lawns and flower beds were now the relics of wartime vegetable gardens, and a natural wilderness had begun to creep in. I walked down to the curious circle of stone beasts and found them mostly toppled. I followed the path through the grove. But I only stood at the edge of the clearing. I would go no nearer Smuggler's Cottage, the place where that serving girl had once been mocked by a false marriage. Nor would anyone have greeted me at the door. Granny Thorne was dead. And it was said, by Finley himself, that her grandson John had gone off to America and had seemed to vanish from the face of the earth.

In my exploring of Whitwell Hall itself, I was slow to mount the narrow steps to the attics. But I was finally drawn to the room where Betty had once lived briefly during her brief life. In this emptiest, loneliest outpost of the house, I met the past face to face, for the garrets where Betty and I had slept were the least changed.

In her room the small chest of drawers, too ample for Betty's few possessions, still stood by the bed. Something led me to the battered chest, and I opened a drawer. It seemed empty, but my hand discovered a bit of cardboard. I drew it out and held it to the light. It was a yellowed photograph. I could make out the two figures, one with an absurd, top-heavy hat. A look of bright, bleak eagerness played about their faces. And I remembered the day when Betty and I had set off for Ventnor in pursuit of an afternoon of freedom for ourselves and a chance at Hubert Sampson for her.

I searched for more in those faces, but they seemed to fade as I scanned them, retreating into the past. Then I shed my only tears over the past.

Whether Lady Eleanor was able to join us or not, Gregory and I dined in some state in the dining room each evening. Finley served us with the averted eyes of an earlier era. I was not to be unmasked by him, for he saw no more than it was his place to see.

This led finally to my doing what Amanda Whitwell would never have thought to do. I paid a visit to the kitchens, drawn there to know who was still there, and who was gone. I wouldn't have been surprised to find Mrs. Buckle and Mrs. Creeth, still locked in battle. But the kitchens were quieter now, in the charge of two vast, matronly figures dressed in identical black beneath their aprons.

I blinked and saw they were Hilda and Hannah. Though not old, they were strangely subdued, and oddly dignified.

At last, one of them noticed me and gasped, "Oh, 'tis Miss Amanda—Mrs. Forrest, as I should say!" She dropped a curtsy, which nearly broke my composure. The other turned and dropped a curtsy too, though which was Hilda and which Hannah, I couldn't tell or remember. That would have been very like the Miss Amanda of old.

Flattered by a visit from the young lady of the house, they soon warmed to local gossip, and in dribs and drabs the familiar names emerged. Mrs. Creeth, "done in" by running a wartime household, had been pensioned off to a cottage in Nettlecombe, where she lived just a turning away from her old enemy, Mrs. Buckle. The pair of them had made it up in their dotage and were now great comforts to each other.

Abel, the footman, had been killed in the war, and I could not remember which of them, Hilda or Hannah, had loved him. Their sober black uniforms might have meant they mourned him equally.

The kitchens were spotless and hung with copper pans that glowed like suns. Hilda and Hannah had left their skittish youth and settled to lifetimes of sober work. And if one was a maiden and the other a widow, it little mattered to them now.

When I bade them good-bye, one of them stopped me to say, "Oh, miss, it was ever such a terrible thing about poor Miranda. The sea takin' her and all. Why, it seems no longer than yesterday when we got the word and couldn't hardly credit it. Gave us the shivers, Miranda's passing did. And Lady Eleanor, she put up ever such a lovely tablet on the church wall, all devoted to Miranda's memory. Wonderful bit of carving it is too. You ought really to see it, miss."

It was perhaps the only thing that would have shaken me. "No," I said, "I don't think I should be able to look at it. It would only sadden me."

They nodded knowingly. "Miranda's happy now, I daresay," one of them sighed.

And I could only nod, agreeing to that, and make my escape. But not before they both dropped final curtsies.

As the time for parting drew near, Lady Eleanor pushed herself beyond her limits to make each fleeting day count against the empty ones to come. We sat on the terrace one day in the last week of our visit so that she could watch the children playing at croquet on the lawn. Throughout the game, Lady Eleanor's white hands, spotted with age, gripped the arms of her chair as her spirit seemed to struggle out of her body to join the children at their play.

This was the time. I couldn't leave my confession to the hurried agony of the last leave-taking. I must tell her the truth, whether or not she knew it already. I must tear away the last veil of deceit so that I would not finally be a liar in her eyes, if she knew. There would be no better time than now for such a task.

I'd planned—rehearsed—nothing, and so there was no proper way to begin. I was not even sure of gaining her attention. Yet I had to begin.

"There is something I must tell you before we leave."

She seemed not to hear me, though her head twitched in slight impatience.

"I cannot go away without—"

"Oh, just look at little Eleanor!" she cut in. "Just see how she has managed to get a ball right through a hoop and is fairly crowing with glee!"

I could not quite give up. I must try once more. "You must hear me out," I said to Lady Eleanor gently. "You must—"

"Hush," she said, and her hand reached across to grip mine. "Hush, my dearest Amanda, for don't you see? I am quite intent upon my grandchildren."